I0592659

SECRET
NOTTE

SECRET NOTTE

The Secret Royals
Book 1

MARIE LONG

Secret Notte
(The Secret Royals, Book 1)

This book is a work of fiction. Any references to historical events, real people, or real places are used fictitiously. Other names, characters, places, and events are products of the author's imagination, and any resemblance to actual events or places or persons, living or dead, is entirely coincidental.

Cover design by Fiona Jayde Media

Printed in the United States of America

10 9 8 7 6 5 4 3 2 1

ISBN: 978-0-9863019-9-5 (paperback)
ISBN: 978-0-9863019-7-1 (eBook)

SECRET
NOTTE

CHAPTER I

THIS IS HORRIBLE!

I stared hopelessly at my seventh failed attempt sketching one of Bellacigna's exquisite lakeside landscapes. I thought for sure I'd found the perfect place to indulge in some artistic practice, but, boy, was I wrong. I was overwhelmed with composition; I didn't know where to begin. As a Summa Cum Laude graduate in Fine Arts, I should've known better. Completing a simple sketch of a tree shouldn't have been this hard.

I wiped my forehead and stared at the back of my arm. The sweat made my skin look like melted chocolate in the late-afternoon sun. My hair was a sweaty mess, too—a curly, kinky, sweaty mess. It would take hours to get it manageable.

Yeah, definitely time for a break.

As I packed up my charcoal pencils and sketchbook, my cell phone buzzed with an incoming message from Trina, my best friend and former college roommate. She'd been sending me messages nonstop since I arrived in Bellacigna from South Carolina four days ago. Being the flirt she was, she'd been hounding me with questions about how many hot European men I'd snagged so far.

One quick peek at the current message confirmed my suspicions, and I shut down the app, letting the message go unanswered. *Meh. I'll call her tonight.*

Children's laughter came from the lake nearby. Little kids and teenagers in their bathing suits jumped from the dock into the dark-blue water. Two old men walked down to the bank with their fishing rods, and a young, handsome couple strode along the edge of the lake, barefoot and arm-in-arm while they talked. They were tourists, all of them, like me. But Bellacigna hadn't been such a lively country up until two years ago.

Recent news and travel review articles had dubbed Bellacigna one of the top five hottest vacation destinations. Tourists arrived in droves, especially young people and celebrities. The more I read about Bellacigna, the more I imagined myself there, no longer in school, but in the scene. Right after graduating, I made it happen.

Unwilling to let the landscape taunt me any longer, I headed back to the lodge. The mid-sized log cabin sat at the bottom of a hill so lush and green, it looked like something straight out of those Irish Spring commercials.

A few tourists lingered near the large cobblestone fireplace in the lodge's main room. It wasn't lit in the dead of July, but I could imagine how cozy the room would be in the winter.

I went to the bar and ordered a cappuccino, ignoring the amused look I received from the barista. What she thought was so funny about me wanting a cappuccino, I didn't know. I needed something to get my creativity going. I scowled at my steaming cup, where the tiny image of a leaf had been expertly drawn in the cream. *Leaves. Trees. I hate drawing trees.* Bob Ross was probably turning in his grave.

Downing my drink, I spotted a large bulletin board posted on a nearby wall. The board was pinned with flyers, calendars, and everything under the sun advertising various activities going on throughout the country. A few tourists stopped in front of it, chatted a bit, then left. My gaze flitted toward the colorful flyers, many written in languages other than English. One flyer in particular caught my eye: a photo of a good-looking man with a strong jaw, smooth olive skin, a shadow of beard, intense eyes and wearing a dark-blue beanie hat and headphones slung around his neck. There was something odd, yet familiar about that man, but I couldn't quite put my finger on what. The word *Notte* was scrawled across the bottom of the picture in a neon-blue techno-style font. Beneath that was information about the club in Alta Rosa, Bellacigna's capital, where he was performing, along with a note about a free open bar for ladies until eleven. Free *open bar? Sold!*

For the few days I'd been vacationing in Bellacigna, I had yet to experience any of the country's nightlife. *Might as well start with the capital city.* According to the maps on my phone, Alta Rosa was a cheap, fifteen-minute train ride from here.

Time to get my dancing shoes ready.

The swift evening ride through Bellacigna's countryside was peaceful and breathtaking. The skies were various deep shades of orange. Wisps of clouds streaked the sky like soft brushstrokes as the sun set behind the rolling hills and distant mountains. Vast farmlands and rural villages dotted the rich landscape. *Never knew such a magical-looking place existed in the world.* The sight was straight out of a children's storybook. The train stopped only twice, at small towns each time, and before I knew it, I'd arrived at Alta Rosa's grand station.

I exited the train and followed the other passengers through a set of frosted-glass double doors. Entering the main concourse, I thought I'd just stepped into a time machine. The station might as well have been a Renaissance cathedral. Gold-trimmed white walls soared up to a domed ceiling; the pristine floor was crafted of polished grey marble. Gilded frames holding portraits of various city landmarks and persons of renown decorated the walls.

I stopped in front of a grand portrait of the king and queen of Bellacigna. A prominent gold plate stretched beneath the portrait proclaimed in numerous languages: The Royal Family Welcomes You to Alta Rosa. I smiled.

I'd sometimes wondered what it would be like to live a life of royalty. It was probably very demanding of duties, with little time for fun, and that just wasn't my style.

Tearing my gaze from the portrait, I headed out of the station and into the busy downtown streets. The bright neon lights from nearby clubs, restaurants, cafés, and upscale shops gave the city an energy I'd never felt before. People, mainly young couples, strolled along the main strip, basking in the nightlife. No one was dressed in flip-flops, khaki shorts, or gaudy shirts. Everywhere I looked, people were decked out in their finest—sparkling cocktail dresses, smart button-down shirts, high-heeled shoes, suits, ties, and glittering jewelry. They were all dressed and ready to take on the town in style.

I passed a closed department store. The red from my reflection against the dark display window caught my peripheral vision. I stopped and stared at myself for a moment before continuing on my way. Red had never been my favorite color, but for a thrift-store find, the dress was one of the most comfortable dresses I owned. Not to mention it was fancy enough to go clubbing in. The neck strap was snug, and the thigh-length dress hugged my faint curves. Paired with matching like-new three-inch heels I'd swiped from the flea market, it transformed me into a true budget model.

But still, compared to the women who were blinging out brighter than Las Vegas, I might as well have been wearing a potato sack.

Well, I came to enjoy myself at a club and get some free drinks, so what do I care about impressing a bunch of strangers?

I approached a rustic-looking building lit with neon green-and-blue lights around its trim. A sign over the entrance flashed the words: CLUB IMPULSO, and the line of patrons stretched halfway down the block. A steady thumping bass beat of techno music filtered out the entrance as the doors opened and closed. Sighing, I took my place at the back of the line then began inching my way forward. *At this rate, I won't get any free drinks.*

Craning my neck, I tried looking toward the front. No one seemed to be checking IDs. *What's the holdup?* I plucked my phone from my clutch purse and sent a quick reply to one of Trina's earlier messages.

"I heard someone say he's not wearing his shades tonight," a woman behind me said.

I glanced over my shoulder at a group of four women with short-short skirts and just-done hair chattering together in a huddle.

"Are you serious?" another woman said in a heavy British accent.

"This is my serious face, Evie." Her red-haired companion made a straight face.

"You mean we might actually get to see those gorgeous green eyes tonight?" the curly-haired one with a too-powdered face said.

The four girls burst into a fit of obnoxious giggling that sparked gag-worthy memories of middle and high school and the endless cliques of popular girls that I never had anything in common with.

I was finally next in line, and the doorman—all six-feet, muscle-bound bit of him—took one glimpse at me, smiled, and opened the door. "Enjoy yourself, signorina," he said.

I shivered. *Wow, what an accent.* And he didn't look half-bad, either. I adored the way the small wisps of his short, curly hair were swept to one side. If this was how attractive all the men are in Alta Rosa, then maybe Trina might be onto something. Perhaps I should've also considered permanently relocating to my vacation spot. Of course, Trina would *love* that.

Hey, you're not here to chase strange foreign men. You're here to relax, I reminded myself. Besides, everyone here looked like celebrities or well-to-do folk bathed in money. *What guy would even bother wasting his time on a no-name commoner like me?* I didn't have the time for relationships anyway.

The inside of the club was mind-blowingly stimulating. Neon lights flashed, swirled, and sparkled amid giant fish tanks built into the walls and columns. Water bubbled from the bottom of the columns, where lights continuously transitioned through various neon pinks, blues, greens, and yellows. Multicolored paper lanterns flickering to the tempo of the hard techno beat were strung along the railings of the upper-level balcony. More lights shined down onto a massive crowded dance floor, and on the raised platform of the deejay booth, a man was posted among mixers and other sound equipment.

I headed for the bar and, after squeezing through crowds of people, managed to get my first free drink of the night. I hoped it wouldn't be the last. Drink in hand, I snaked through the crowd, moving my body to the beat. I paused to casually sip and savor my beloved Amaretto. I looked out into the crowd, mostly women, huddled before the stage, waving and dancing wildly, trying to get the deejay's attention. And the deejay looked exactly like the guy on the flyer, sans the sunglasses. Too focused in his work, he didn't pay the fawning girls any mind. I might have dared to say he was mouth-watering. *Must be those headphones around his neck. Or maybe that one top button undone on his satin shirt.*

No wonder the girls were clamoring for his attention. I bet he got that kind of treatment every day. *What kind of life is that, always being pestered like that?*

But the music he played—wow. It possessed me, urging me to dance. I found myself inching closer to the stage, my body once again rocking to the techno beat. I took another sip of Amaretto, which calmed my nerves as the sweet liquor slid down my throat. A roar of swoons rippled from the foot of the stage, and dozens of female arms reached toward the deejay booth. Four suited burly men with dark sunglasses posted themselves in front of the stage, their arms crossed, keeping the fanatic women at bay. I shook my head at the senseless chaos and looked toward DJ Notte to see his reaction. Two piercing eyes were looking back in my direction. The more I stared, the more I tried to remember where I'd seen them— *him*—before. The thoughts took me back years ago, back when I was a sophomore in high school. But that was when the memory ended.

I took another sip, trying to clear my head. The thoughts didn't make sense, and the more I tried to comprehend them, the more my head started to hurt, so I just dismissed them. Realizing I had been staring at DJ Notte for far too long, I was about to tear my gaze from him when he quickly averted his eyes to the girls down front. He smiled and nodded at them then focused once more on working his mixer.

What was that all about? I brought my drink to my lips, only to discover that the glass was empty. Frowning, I looked around for a place to set it down.

A charming man dressed in a fine suit and bowtie approached, holding a tray of discarded glasses and beer mugs. Smiling, he held out his hand, and I gave him my glass. He looked about my age, with wavy black hair and smooth creamy skin. He was tall, athletically built, and absolutely delicious. *Geez. Are all the Bellacignan guys this attractive?* This place was almost too perfect; it was starting to scare me.

I hung out at the club for a few hours, dancing, enjoying the music, sipping more Amaretto, and watching more drunk fangirls make fools of themselves. Around midnight, DJ Notte wrapped up his set, packed up his laptop, and left with the four men in suits. Another deejay came out on stage and set up in his place. He, too, was cute, but apparently not cute enough to have a flock of inebriated girls stalking him.

Notte had me intrigued, and I wondered if he was on his way to another club gig, so I followed him. Exiting the club, I noticed Notte was already gone. *That was quick!* There was no telling where he could be in this huge city, so I decided to call it a night. I eyed the line of taxis parked along the sidewalk all the way down the street. The activity downtown was winding down as the hour drew on.

I started for a bright-yellow cab, but a couple shoved past me and hopped inside. My nose wrinkled at the smell of too much alcohol coming off them. I frowned then sighed, watching the cab drive off.

My feet were on fire. Doing another club was definitely not a good idea, and I did *not* want to walk the seven blocks back to the train station in heels. But as more people left the clubs looking about to fall over at any second, I knew they needed those cabs more than I did.

I looked down at the sidewalk and noticed just how clean it was—everything in the city was immaculate. The ground was so clean, in fact, that I did what any sensible woman with aching feet would do—took off my shoes and walked barefoot. *Relief!* The concrete was cold, but it was nothing compared to the pain caused from all the dancing. With my shoes in one hand and my purse clutched under my other arm, I quickly backtracked my path toward the train station. A few people I passed looked my way, staring with arched eyebrows, snooty glares, and turned-up noses, but I didn't care. *When a woman's got sore feet, she has to do what she has to do.*

I stopped at a crosswalk and watched the sea of cabs and fancy cars whoosh by. The sound of glass shattering in the distance followed by two men's voices startled me. I looked farther down the street but saw only pedestrians walking to and fro. *Must be that time of night when the drunks came out and play.* Every city seemed to have them.

The Walk signal flashed, and I hustled across the street. The two men's voices grew louder as I continued toward the next city block. One man yelled sharp, angry Italian phrases, and the other man stammered over his words.

The two men stood on the curb alongside a parked limo. A black sedan was parked in front of the limo. One of the men next to the limo stood taller than the other. As I passed them, I glimpsed the tall man and nearly did a double take. That pair of black shades perched atop his dark-blue beanie hat immediately caught my attention. And that single top button on his satin shirt was still undone. Intense green eyes met mine. My heart gave a small nervous flutter. *That can't be…*

I couldn't tear my gaze away. It *was* him—DJ Notte, without his fangirls. Notte's gaze faltered a moment, then his eyes widened. Surprise and concern replaced his expression of rage.

His mouth dropped open, and before I knew it, he lunged in my direction, his hand extended. "Wait, signorina!"

Startled, I stepped forward, and a sudden sharp pain shot through my foot, all the way up the back of my leg. I stumbled, feeling my balance giving way, and more pain rushed through my other foot. I dropped my purse and shoes. The pain wouldn't stop. Then my body suddenly felt weightless. I shut my eyes, my heart sinking into my stomach. The scent of sandalwood surrounded me, and I felt the heat and rigidness of another body against mine. Opening my eyes, I stared up at a man with a concerned, emerald-green gaze, a set jaw, and a hint of a wrinkle in his brow. His mouth opened slowly, as if he were about to say something, and I caught a glimpse of his pearly whites. He closed his mouth and looked over his shoulder at the other man, who was older with greying hair. "Now look what you have done, Filippo!"

Filippo cringed and muttered something under his breath in a language that sounded like Italian. "I'll clean it up right away." He brushed past us and knelt where I'd dropped my purse and shoes—in a mass of broken glass. The jagged-edged top half of a wine bottle lay among the glass, its dark contents spilled into a puddle on the sidewalk.

A deep growl rumbled from Notte's throat, and my body stiffened. "Leave not one single shard or drop of wine on that sidewalk, *capisce*?"

"*Sì*, Your Grace…"

Your Grace? Is this guy a deejay or a noble?

Notte walked toward the sedan parked in front of the limo. A man in a dark suit and glasses hopped out of the driver's side, rushed around, and opened the back door.

"Vittorio. To the hospital at once," Notte said.

I slowly came to my senses. "Whoa, wait... hospital? What's going on? Put me down. I'm not going anywhere."

Notte looked back at me apologetically and shook his head. "*Scusi*, but glass shards are lodged deep in the bottoms of your feet, and you are bleeding badly. It is best that we seek medical attention, lest the wounds get worse."

Blood. Glass. Hospitals. Ugh. My head was spinning, and my feet were numb. Before I could make up my mind, Notte laid me in the backseat of the sedan.

"Wait... my purse..." I muttered.

"Filippo will meet us at the hospital shortly with your items, signorina," Notte said. He sat with me and placed my feet on his lap. Blood from the wounds dribbled onto his pants, creating deep crimson spots. The car jerked forward, and the passing city lights illuminated the interior, flashing across Notte's face.

I tried to sit up, but pain shot through my calves. I wondered if I'd lost a lot of blood already.

Frowning, he rubbed the tops of my feet. I really wished my feet weren't numb, or else I might've actually enjoyed it.

"W-What are you doing?" I asked, looking at our awkward position.

"Your feet need to be elevated. Do not worry, signorina. We will be at the hospital soon."

I cringed. "Your pants are ruined."

"I can always get new pants. Right now, my main priority is you."

The way he said that in such a concerned, yet determined tone sent a slight shiver down my spine. I'd gone from getting a couple of drinks to getting medical attention. *Geez, this is* not *the way I want to end the night.* "You're DJ Notte, right?" *Great going, Claudia. What kind of question was that?*

He smiled, revealing more of those pearly whites. "Call me Stefano."

"Okay… Stefano."

"And you are?"

"Claudia."

His smile grew as he studied me closely. "Claudia. *Bella.*"

Another tingle of delight traveled down my spine and to my fingertips as he uttered my name with that delightful accent. *Maybe tonight won't end so bad, after all.*

CHAPTER 2

THE LIMO SCREECHED TO A HALT AT THE entrance to the emergency room of the Alta Rosa hospital. Filippo hopped out, hustled around the car, and opened the back door. Stefano scooped me up in his arms and carried me to the entrance.

"I can walk, you know," I protested.

"Not with those feet, you cannot," Stefano said.

I rolled my eyes then heard a nagging voice in my head. *Why are you even complaining? You're being carried around in the arms of a hot guy, for goodness' sake!*

19

Strangely, but not surprising, that nagging voice sounded a lot like Trina's.

We headed inside, and Stefano flagged down a nurse. She looked our way and halted in her tracks. Her eyes grew wider than saucers as she rushed toward us. She spoke some frantic Italian then suddenly paused, took one look at my feet, and gasped. Sweeping past the receptionist's station, she quickly muttered something to a man sitting there then disappeared through a pair of double doors that lay beyond the station. The receptionist got up from the desk, asked for my name and info, and transcribed it onto a form attached to a clipboard. Moments later, a gurney surged through the doors, accompanied by two more nurses. Stefano transported me to the gurney, and one of the nurses propped my feet on a pillow. Blood soaked through the pillow, staining the perfectly white pillowcase. The receptionist handed the clipboard to one of the nurses, who tucked it in a small side pocket on the gurney. As the nurses wheeled me off, Stefano walked beside me.

The dim, warm lights of the main concourse gave way to blinding lights as we entered a large room with several other gurneys lining the walls. Most of the gurneys were occupied, and three nurses scrambled to and fro, tending to each patient. The air was thick with sickness and despair. It made my skin prickle.

Two of the nurses scattered, gathering first-aid items, while one stayed and took my vitals. When she finished, Stefano said something to her in Italian while gesturing to me. She looked at me and nodded. They chatted back and forth for a bit, then she gathered the other nurses.

Stefano placed his hand on my shoulder and smiled. His soft touch was warm and reassuring.

I nervously smiled back at him. Confusion flooded my mind. "What did you say to that nurse?"

"You are getting a private room."

Private room? Over a few little cuts? This is too much. And I knew I wouldn't be able to afford whatever hospital bills might come with special treatment. "No, I don't need a private room. Really. Can't the doctor just do what they need to do here?"

Stefano's gaze darkened. "Claudia, your injury was the fault of my careless assistant. That reflects on me. Therefore, I will see that my errors are rectified to the very best of my ability. I will ensure you receive the best care and comfort while you are here."

"A private room sounds expensive. I'll never be able to afford all this." I shuddered at the thought, trying to add up the costs in my head. *Staying in a fancy private room for ten minutes: three thousand dollars. Getting blood on the pillowcases: three hundred*

*dollars a pillow. Getting both feet treated by the doctor:
five thousand dollars per foot, plus an extra five hundred
dollars per glass shard removed from each foot... Bye-bye,
life savings.*

Stefano laughed. "Nonsense. Bellacigna offers
free universal healthcare."

I blinked. *Free healthcare? Wow.* I'd never heard
those two words uttered in the same sentence before.

The nurses returned and wheeled me out of the
large room, up an elevator to the fourth floor, down
a lighted hallway, and into a small, quiet room. The
air smelled crisp and fresh, unlike the musty, skin-
crawling despair of the emergency room. Framed oil
paintings of vineyards, mountains, and lush green
hills reminiscent of Bellacigna's countryside hung
from the cream-colored walls. A vase containing an
assortment of fresh multicolored roses sat on a side
table next to the bed.

Stefano sat on a comfortable-looking blue-plaid
couch against the far wall under the large window
overlooking the city. He scooted to the edge, holding
one of the couch's blue accent pillows, and watched
me intently. *Is he worried about me?*

Two of the nurses transported me to the bed
while the head nurse—whose nametag said Elena—
washed her hands at a tiny sink built into the wall on
the opposite end of the room. The bed felt softer
than a cloud as I sank into it. My feet were propped

on several pillows, and the nurses gathered around, wheeling a table of supplies next to them. With a nod of her head, Elena shooed the other two away. As soon as they left, Stefano hopped up from the couch and stood at my bedside.

"You will be just fine, Signorina Gray," Elena said, sliding on a pair of latex gloves. She got right to work, cleaning the wounds with alcohol and plucking out the glass shards with a pair of tweezers. I winced each time she pulled, making my feet tingle with an eerie, unpleasant sensation.

Stefano rested a hand on my shoulder, and I relaxed. I studied his face again, hoping to remember something about him, but I still couldn't recollect. Maybe I was mistaking him for someone else.

When the last shard of glass was gone, Elena cleaned the wounds again, smeared antiseptic cream on them, then applied bandages. She secured the bandages with medical tape, which she wrapped around my foot. "It is a good thing the glass did not go in too deep," Elena said. "You will not need stitches."

"*Bene*," Stefano said, relief spreading across his face.

"So does that mean I can go now?" I asked.

Elena held up one finger. "*Un momento.* I will confirm with the doctor." She grabbed a folder from the table and hurried out the door.

An uneasy silence filled the room as Stefano and I waited. I looked at him, and he looked back at me, a hint of a smile on his face.

"So, this might sound weird, but I feel like we've met before," I finally said.

His eyebrows rose then pinched as he stared at me intently. "Perhaps. Now that you mention it, I feel as though I know you, too."

Then, just like that, the memories came to me. "There was this boy back in high school. He looked a little like you and spoke with a similar accent. I think he was a foreign exchange student for about half the semester. Man, he was cute." Feeling my cheeks get hot, I added quickly, "Uh, not to mention an amazing artist and musician. I think... his name was... Santi?"

His expression returned to surprise. "Wait. Are you the same Claudia Gray who sat two rows in front of me in Ms. Davidson's art class?"

My mouth dropped open. "Uh... yeah?"

He beamed. "*Che meraviglia!*"

"Wait... so Santi was you?"

"Sì. Santi is my middle name. That was the way my parents enrolled me during the short time I attended. Oh, I am so happy to see you again, Claudia."

Who would've thought I'd run into my old classmate here in this faraway place? We were never really close friends or anything, but I'd stood up to a group of immature juniors who were playing pranks on him just for being a foreign exchange student.

If I hadn't known better, I would've thought Stefano was blushing a little. "So you live here in this awesome country? And you're a deejay?"

He chuckled. "Sì. Among other things."

As we talked, just like old times, happiness swept over me. But it quickly disappeared as a woman with short dark hair entered the room. Draped over her white overcoat was a bright-green stethoscope. Carrying the same folder Elena had, she stopped at my bed and smiled at us.

"*Ciao*. I am Rossana." She scanned the folder then looked at Stefano. "I was surprised to hear that you were here in the hospital, Your Grace. It was a relief to know that you were not the patient."

Stefano gave her a half smile. "Sì. But not so fortunate for my dear friend, Claudia." His gaze shifted back to me.

My heart fluttered. *Dear friend? Is that what he considers me?* Nothing really happened between us back then, other than that one little incident with the bullies. Beyond working as partners in art class, I'd barely talked to him. Maybe over time we might've become more than just friends if he hadn't moved back to his home country halfway into the semester.

Rossana looked up from her folder. "You are free to go, Signorina Gray. But I do advise you to stay off your feet for a few days. No hiking, running, dancing, *et cetera*. And do be sure to wear some comfortable shoes."

"So no high heels," I said with a sigh.

Rossana laughed. "*Definitely* no high heels."

Sounds like I'll be shut up in bed for the rest of the week. What a lousy vacation it was turning out to be.

"*Grazie*, Rossana," Stefano said. "I will make sure she is well cared for."

I looked at him, my eyebrows raised. *What does he mean by that?*

Rossana nodded. "Okay. Well, then, I will be off. Have a good night—or should I say morning?" She turned and left.

I glanced at the fancy-looking mahogany clock hanging on the wall opposite the bed. It was almost three o'clock.

Stefano leaned over the bed. "Ready to go?"

The way he hovered near me made my heart race. The heat of his body so close to mine was inviting. I gulped and nodded. "Y-Yeah, sure. Let me walk, please."

Stefano shook his head. "You heard the doctor. You need to stay off your feet. I will get you a wheelchair."

"Oh c'mon. It was just a couple of cuts. Not like I'm decrepit or something."

"Would you rather I carry you instead?"

I wasn't sure if I should have been happy or embarrassed that Stefano was willing to carry me around like a helpless child. I could already hear Trina nagging me. She would probably think I'd totally lost it if I told her about everything.

I was suddenly lifted off my feet, and I started. "What are you doing!"

He chuckled. "You took too long to answer."

I had no choice but to give in to his insistence. Stefano happily carried me through the hospital. We received smiles and stares from a few passersby, but Stefano paid them no mind.

The sliding-glass doors of the emergency room entrance slid open, and Bellacigna's warm summer air whisked over my face. I inhaled the fresh air, trying to shake the dreariness of the hospital from my system.

"All right. So what am I going to owe you in return?" I asked.

Stefano arched an eyebrow. "What do you mean?"

"Don't get me wrong, I'm eternally grateful that you've helped me like this, but let's be real here. Nothing in this world is ever free. My mama always told me that."

His gaze went rigid. "You owe me nothing, Claudia. I take full responsibility for your accident."

Nothing about the situation felt right, unless he was paying me back for saving him all those years ago.

Stefano looked up, beyond me. I followed his gaze to Filippo's black sedan, which was parked right where we'd seen it last, with the limo parked behind it. Filippo and Vittorio were standing next to the cars, talking. As Stefano approached, they stopped and looked our way. Filippo scrambled to the back door of the limo, while Vittorio hopped in the driver's seat of the sedan.

Stefano cast Filippo a cold stare as he helped me into the limo. "Did you clean up that mess?"

"Sì, Your Grace," Filippo said with a curt nod. "Every last piece."

"And the lady's things?"

"Her items are in the back, Your Grace."

"*Bene.*"

I shifted into a comfortable position in the backseat and propped my feet up on the opposite seat. Next to my feet were my purse and shoes. With a sigh of relief, I grabbed my purse and checked inside. All of my ID and money were still there, thank goodness.

"Do you have everything?" Stefano asked, the closeness of his voice startling me. He sat right next to me. Filippo closed the back door and hopped into the driver's seat.

"Yes," I said.

"*Ottimo.* Then shall I take you home?"

"Please."

After a beat, Stefano smiled. "And where might that be?"

A few seconds later, I realized what he was asking, then I slapped my forehead. "Oh, sorry. I'm at the Verdi Colline Lodge. Just a few miles outside of Cittàcigni."

He blinked. "Cittàcigni?"

I nodded, curious about his reaction.

"Why... I live in that city." He leaned over to the opposite seat and snapped his fingers, getting Filippo's attention. They chatted briefly in Italian, and Filippo put the car in gear and we were off. Vittorio followed us.

"Talk about coincidence," I said. "So I guess you know where that lodge is, huh?"

"I do. I go there a lot in the winter to ski. It is a popular Bellacignan activity."

"Huh. Well, this Southern girl prefers her feet to be in a pair of warm, fuzzy boots in the winter—not on two wooden sticks, thank you."

He stared at me for a moment then let out a cute and invigorating laugh. "You can still make me laugh. Still the same wonderful girl I remember."

He talks as if we were life-long friends. I'm starting to wonder if maybe he has me confused with someone else. I smiled back at him. "So what's with all this 'Your Grace' stuff?"

His smile faded. "It is just a title. A status. I prefer to just be called Stefano."

"So does this mean you're some kind of noble or royal prince or something?"

He kept a straight face. "I prefer to just be seen as a young man named Stefano."

The way he dodged the questions made me wonder what he was really hiding.

"Hey." Stefano touched my chin with his fingers, which felt soft and cool. He gently tilted my head up, forcing me to look at him. "I am sorry if I sounded cold or off-putting. I just want people to see me for me. Can *you* at least do that, Claudia?"

Though I willed my eyes to look elsewhere, they remained fixated on him. I absently moistened my bottom lip with my tongue and whispered, "Y-Yeah…"

Stefano's eyes moved down slightly and narrowed. He withdrew his hand from my face and looked up, beyond me.

We rode in silence for several minutes. I stared out the window, watching the city pass by as my mind spun. I'd gone from being carried around in the arms of a hot guy to riding in the backseat of a limo with a hot guy. Trina would have absolutely died if she were there.

"Are you just visiting Bellacigna?" Stefano asked, breaking the silence.

I looked over at him, relieved he'd taken the initiative to strike up a conversation. "Uh, yeah. I'm here for a month."

He studied me with enticing green eyes. "Do you still live in South Carolina?"

"Yep, Columbia."

"Well, I bid you a formal welcome to my home country of Bellacigna." He smiled.

"Yeah, what a welcome." Trying to hide my smile, I pointed to my feet.

"That will never happen again. You have my word."

"That accident was just as much my fault. I should've looked where I was going." *But I was too focused on you.* I looked away, trying to dismiss the thought from my mind.

"There is not much to do in the Cittàcigni outskirts that does not require walking or climbing."

I groaned. "I'll probably just stay in my room for a few days and work on some sketches."

"Ah, so you are still drawing?" His expression brightened.

I scrunched my face. "Yeah, though I've been having a stroke of artist's block recently. That's what brought me to Alta Rosa. I needed to clear my head, get some motivation and inspiration, and have a little fun."

"There is so much to do in this country. I can show you around sometime."

"That's sweet. Maybe I'll take you up on that offer later."

He gave me a wry smile.

"I was hoping to run into a celebrity or two while I was here. Didn't think one of them would be a famous deejay."

He laughed. "Famous deejay? I just do it for fun."

"Oh yeah? Then what about all those girls fawning over you?"

He stopped laughing and looked at me seriously. "Those girls do not like me for my music."

I raised my eyebrows then remembered our previous conversation. "Oh, I get it. They're gold diggers."

He wrinkled his brow. "Gold… diggers?"

"Yeah, you know. Women who strive to marry wealthy men in order to extract money from them."

He nodded in understanding. "Ah, sì. Many of them sound exactly like that."

He sounded perhaps ashamed of his wealth. Maybe unhappy. I'd heard the horror stories of rich people being unhappy. "It must be terrible for you, having to deal with that every day."

"Eh." He shrugged. "It has its ups and downs. I would not call my life privileged in the way you may think. It is... very exhausting." He fell silent and stared out his window.

I did the same. There wasn't much to see once we were out of the city. Soft, faint moonlight covered the dark countryside all around us. The limo started to slow down as we approached the lodge. We pulled right up to the entrance. Filippo hopped out, ran around back, and opened the door.

Stefano, not budging, looked at me intently. "Claudia, would you like to have lunch with me tomorrow? Maybe dinner?"

I opened my mouth to speak, but no coherent words came out. *Did he just ask me out?* My ears were definitely deceiving me. It was late, and my brain was half-awake, so I was pretty sure I'd misinterpreted what he'd really said. "Uh..."

His eyes glinted with amusement. "Whatever you decide, let me know." He fished into his pants pocket and pulled out a business card. Holding it between his index and middle finger, he handed it to me.

I took the card. Aside from the extravagant image of his deejay name inside the outline of a raven, the card also had his phone number and e-mail address on it.

Stefano got out of the car and extended his hand. I gathered my belongings and scooted carefully out of the car. Before my feet could hit the ground, Stefano picked me up again and carried me in his arms.

My heart sank into my gut. "Whoa. Wait. I'm fine here. I can walk to my room."

"You do not have suitable shoes at the moment, Claudia. Let me at least carry you inside so you do not have to walk in all this dirt."

He had a point, so I complied. As soon as we crossed the threshold, he set me down on the smooth wood floors of the lodge. It sure was nice to be able to walk on my own again, even though my feet did sting a little when I put weight on them. I tried to play it cool around Stefano, not wanting to give him any reason to carry me all the way to my room.

"I'm fine, now. Thank you for everything."

He inclined his head. "The pleasure was all mine. I hope that I will see you again, soon."

I sucked in a breath. "Yeah... maybe..."

He turned to the door. "*Arrivederci*, Claudia. Pleasant dreams."

As I watched him return to the limo, I pulled the business card from my purse. His phone number stared back at me. The scent of sandalwood cologne teased my senses. As tempting as his offer was, I had to remind myself why I was here. My sketchbooks weren't going to sketch themselves. And if I ever expected to get a good-paying job after this vacation, I needed to focus on perfecting my craft.

With that thought, I stuffed the card into my purse, promising to forget about it tomorrow, and headed to my room.

CHAPTER 3

THE OBNOXIOUS RINGING OF THE PHONE ON MY nightstand woke me up the next day. I rolled over in bed and reached for the receiver. "Hullo?"

"*Buongiorno*, Signorina Gray," a lady said in a professional, accented voice. "You have a small parcel at the front desk."

At that point, I was fully awake. "What?" I'd told only Trina and my parents where I was staying. *They wouldn't be sending me mail here, would they?* "I think there's some mistake."

"The parcel is addressed to Signorina Claudia Gray."

I pursed my lips. The clock on the nightstand said 11:30. Well, I needed an excuse to get up, anyway. After hanging up the phone, I swung my legs off the bed. About to place my feet on the floor, I suddenly remembered the night before.

It had been sweet of Stefano to pamper me the way he had. But I wanted no part of the fast-paced life of fame and money that he apparently led. Money made people do crazy things. I'd seen enough of it from all the TV celebrities. Besides, with all those girls chasing Stefano, he'd probably given me no more than a fleeting thought.

I needed to do the same. *It's a new day. Time to try creating a decent sketch.* I slowly placed my feet on the cool wooden floor and closed my eyes, anticipating pain, but there was none. I opened my eyes again. Surely, the wounds hadn't healed *that* soon. It wasn't until I stood that the pain came, but thankfully, it had lessened to an agitating pain that would beg me to sit down and prop my feet up on a nice soft pillow. At least I could walk.

I took a cold, refreshing shower, which seemed to feel even better on my feet. Then I got dressed and applied new bandages to them. Afterward, I slid into a pair of my most comfortable sneakers, grabbed my room key, and left.

It was past noon by the time I arrived at the front desk. Only a few people sat around the main room, but most were converged at the café for lunch.

"*Buongiorno*. How may I help you?" the female desk attendant said.

I looked around for any stray packages. "Uh... I was notified of a parcel for Claudia Gray."

Her eyes brightened. "Ah, sì. *Un momento.*" She turned and disappeared through a door, where I spotted suitcases, hanging clothes carriers, and taped-up boxes. She returned moments later with a shallow, powder-blue rectangular box secured with thin twine. A label stuck on the front of the box was addressed in elegant calligraphy. As I held the box closer, a sweet smell wafted from it. I inhaled deeply. I knew that smell—jasmine.

I returned to my room as quickly as my feet would allow. Sitting on the edge of my bed, the box in my lap, I tugged at the string and let it fall to the floor. I slowly opened the package. Underneath neatly folded tissue paper was a bunch of white jasmine flowers, still fresh.

My mouth dropped open. *Flowers? Who in the—* I caught sight of something beneath the flowers: a card. I flipped it open and read carefully.

"Dear Claudia, It was very refreshing to see you again. I wish you good health and a speedy recovery, and I look forward to meeting you again very soon.

Sincerely yours, S. T.

P.S. I still await your answer about lunch or dinner."

I must have read the note a hundred times, wondering if it was real. I was an artist and the ultimate introvert. Occurrences like last night's accident were exactly why I didn't go out often. *No one* ever bought me flowers or wrote me notes. I wasn't *that* privileged to be swept up by an admirer just yet.

Enclosed with the note was a "Permanent VIP" ticket that granted me free access to all of DJ Notte's shows, as well as free drinks. *Unbelievable...* I shook my head. Stefano's gestures were sweet—maybe a little too sweet. He'd gone way beyond repaying me for a kindness all those years ago. I inhaled the flowers a final time, savoring their succulent scent, then placed them back in the box. I didn't know what I was going to say to him if we ended up meeting again. I definitely didn't want to lead him on to something that probably could never be. He was cute. He was attentive. He was a gentleman. He was the kind of man I wanted in my life. But no man was perfect. Stefano most likely carried baggage that he hid well. Maybe that was why he was being so nice.

I guess it wouldn't hurt to get to know him a little more, even if I only had less than four weeks left of my vacation.

However, I was determined to get some sketches done first. I grabbed my art supply bag and headed out the door. I ordered a cappuccino to go, and returned to the same spot by the lake. *I'll sketch those trees if it kills me!*

The area was busy with tourists, as usual, but the noise didn't distract me. My mind bounced between sketching trees and Stefano.

I shook out of my thoughts and stared at my sketchbook page. The scene of the countryside had sprung to life. The trees were perfect. Finally, I'd sketched one worthy of being added to my portfolio. I wanted to keep drawing for as long as the artist bug was biting, so I turned to a fresh page of my sketchbook and let my right hand do the work.

I finished the second sketch and let out a triumphant sigh. Checking the time on my phone, I realized it was almost four o'clock. *Have I really been out here for over three hours?*

A shadow suddenly appeared on the page. Feeling another presence so close, I sucked in a breath and slowly looked over my shoulder. The first thing I saw was a pair of expensive-looking sports shoes. My gaze traveled up along a pair of fitted black jeans and a dark-grey button-down shirt then stopped at the face of a man sporting a shadow of beard covering a hard jawline. Intense green eyes looked back at me.

Stefano. I smiled.

"*Buongiorno*, Claudia." He brushed aside strands of curly black hair that spilled out from under his beanie hat.

"H-Hi," I said in a cracked voice then swallowed. "What are you doing here?"

"I stopped by to see how you were faring." He glanced at my sketchpad, his eyes widening slightly. "You drew that?"

"Drew what?" I followed his gaze and did a double take at the image of a jasmine flower I'd sketched. My mind had been everywhere, and I hadn't been aware of what I was drawing. "Oh, uh, yeah."

"*Bellissimo*, Claudia! Your work looks so professional."

I flushed. "I'm trying to build up my portfolio so I'll have something worthwhile to show when I go job hunting."

"Whoever would dare turn you down is a fool."

I chuckled. "If only it were that easy. It's a competitive market out there, especially for a grad student like me."

He sprawled out next to me on the grass, leaning back on an elbow. "Grad student?"

I nodded. "Well… grad-school graduate. This vacation was a celebration present to myself."

"I see."

"What about you?"

"I did my college years at Alta Rosa University. I wish I could take vacations sometimes."

I arched an eyebrow. "A vacation from this place? Are you insane? This is the most beautiful country in the world!"

He smiled. "It is, but sometimes I like to get away from the stresses of life." He paused and stared out at the lake, where a group of teenaged boys jumped in and splashed each other. He looked back at me. "I am still waiting for you to accept or decline my offer, Claudia. It is too late for lunch, so I guess it would have to be dinner."

His offer. I'd been so caught up in my own work, I'd forgotten. Perhaps after today's artistic success, I could afford to reward myself. "All right. Dinner it is."

CHAPTER 4

I MESSAGED STEFANO, LETTING HIM KNOW TO come get me around seven in the evening. It was five minutes before seven when I stepped outside the lodge in a pair of skinny jeans, a button-down blouse, and comfortable flats. A black sedan was parked out front, and Stefano and Vittorio leaned up against the hood, chatting. Stefano was the first to spot me, and on cue, he swept to my side, while Vittorio opened the rear passenger's door.

Stefano looked me over and smiled. "You look exquisite, Claudia."

"Thank you," I said, inclining my head.

He gave me another once-over, stopping at my feet. His brow pinched. "Are you sure those shoes are comfortable for you?"

I frowned. *Is he going to keep asking me about my feet all night?* "Yes, I appreciate your concern. I'm fine, really. I haven't been walking around all that much today as it is, so let me walk now, please."

His lips pursed, and he exhaled through his nose. "Very well." He nodded and held out his arm.

I graciously accepted his gesture and hooked my arm with his. He escorted me to the car, where Vittorio waited patiently, holding open the back door. Vittorio kept a hard and stoic expression beneath a pair of dark shades that made him look more like a bodyguard or FBI agent from the movies. He wasn't bald, at least, or else he would have fit that stereotype perfectly.

Stefano helped me in the car before climbing in to settle onto the plush velvet seat. Vittorio shut the door behind him and got into the driver's seat.

"I guess it would be appropriate for me to ask what kind of food you like." Stefano ran his fingers through his hair in an adorable way.

I noticed a hint of red on his cheeks. *What's he so embarrassed about?* "Well, being the Southern girl I am, I have a firm liking to mac 'n cheese, fried chicken, collard greens, candied yams, ham hocks, baked beans, apple dumplings… oh, sweet tea. Can't ever forget the sweet tea." I chuckled.

Stefano laughed as well. "Ah, I do remember the first time you introduced me to ham hocks."

I raised my eyebrows. "You do?"

"Sì. You brought some in during lunch period. Your mother had stewed a giant pot for dinner the night before. I will admit, it was tasty."

"Mama cooks the best ham hocks. I can't believe you remembered that."

He grinned. "I have never forgotten the moments we spent together in high school, Claudia."

I moistened my lips. *Wow, for the few times we'd interacted, this guy's got a memory better than an elephant's.*

His gaze faltered briefly. "Would you… like to try some popular Bellacignan dishes?"

"I'd love to. What restaurant are we going to?"

Stefano's gaze shifted to his window, and he cleared his throat. "No public restaurant. I was thinking more of a quiet private dinner at my estate."

I blinked. "Wait—what? *Estate?*" I instinctively grazed my fingers over the door handle, only to realize the car was moving and we were already on the road. "Wait, no. I'm not going to anyone's estate."

Stefano studied me for a moment, then his eyes fell to my hand. His Adam's apple bobbed, and he lowered his head. "*Scusi*. I did not mean to offend or upset you. I should have asked."

I sighed and let my fingers slide away from the handle. He seemed sincere enough, but that didn't stop my nerves that were surging through my brain. "Look, Stefano. You're sweet and all, and I appreciate everything you did for me last night, but you're starting to get a little forward. I mean, this is the first time in, like, ten years since we've seen each other. And I'm not ready to get whisked away to some strange home in a foreign country. If you don't want to do a restaurant, then let's return to the lodge and talk over a cup of coffee or something."

He closed his eyes, put his hands up in a praying position, and brought them to his lips. He inclined his head. "You have my deepest, most sincere apologies, Claudia. Please forgive me."

I raised my eyebrows. *Is he actually begging my forgiveness?* I reached out for his hand. "Hey, you don't have to do all that. I forgive you. Just... be more careful next time, okay?"

He opened his eyes.

I paused and looked at our hands. His skin was smooth and warm. The touch electrified the pads of my fingertips. I quickly let go.

A hint of a grateful smile touched his lips. "Very well, Claudia. A restaurant it is. I know a place."

My body relaxed a bit. "Okay."

Stefano took out his phone from an inner pocket in his blazer. "*Un momento.* I need to make a phone call." He lifted his head and said something in Italian to Vittorio.

"Sì," Vittorio replied then turned down the nearest street.

Stefano returned to his phone conversation.

When he ended the call, I asked, "What restaurant are we going to?"

"It is called La Porta del Duca, a family-owned *ristorante.* Popular for its eggplant croquettes." He quirked a smile. "They are... undeniably addicting."

I smiled. "Oh? Well that sounds interesting to try. Never had eggplant before."

"I think you will like it." His cell buzzed, and he fished it out of his blazer. He took one look at the screen, scowled, and muttered under his breath.

He sighed, looking at me apologetically, then answered the phone. His conversation with the mysterious caller grew more intense as the veins in his neck became visible. Finally, he ended the call and stuffed it back into his pocket as he muttered more obscenities.

"Is everything okay?" I asked with raised eyebrows.

He leaned back against the seat and ran his hand through his hair in that adorable way again. "Sì, just my father. I swear, he will not give me a moment of peace."

"Let me guess: overbearing parent?"

"It is complicated." He opened his mouth as if to say more but closed it quickly. "No need to worry about that. Let us just enjoy the rest of the day."

Vittorio drove into Cittàcigni and turned down a less-busy cobblestone street. At the end of the slightly bumpy ride was a quaint, ivy-covered, two-story brick building. A few wrought-iron tables and chairs sat outside the building. A wood sign framed with matching wrought iron and the words *La Porta del Duca* hung above the front door, flapping in a light, passing breeze. Several cars, including a few expensive-looking ones and a limo, were parked outside the building along the curb all the way down the street. It didn't look like we were going to be able to park, but then Vittorio turned down a hidden driveway through a veil of hanging ivy. On the side of the building, Vittorio parked in an empty spot near a door.

"Now that's pretty cool. Having your own private parking lot like this," I said.

Stefano smiled. Without waiting for Vittorio, he opened the back door and let himself out. I followed.

"This parking area is reserved for family members." Stefano extended his hand to me. "Come, Claudia. This way to the private dining area."

I took his hand, and he led me up a set of stairs and through the side door. The mixed smells of pasta, chicken, vegetables, and spices wafted all around, and I realized we were in the kitchen. All the cooks and wait staff stopped what they were doing and acknowledged us with polite nods.

Stefano returned the gesture, a slight look of annoyance in his eyes. We exited the kitchen, rounded a corner to another door, and were outside again. But instead of a parking lot, it was a beautiful courtyard. A lone, wrought-iron dinette for two sat under a wood awning with ivy that grew between the spaces and draped down elegantly. White Christmas lights strung between the rooftops created a canopy of glittering stars. A flower-lined pebbled walkway snaked throughout the courtyard and around a fountain, which sat in the middle. The steady trickle of the fountain's waterfall was like a soothing melody.

"This is beautiful," I said breathlessly.

Smiling, Stefano pulled out a chair for me. "I am pleased that you like it. I hope you will also enjoy the food." When I was seated, he took his place across from me. A waiter clad in black and wearing an apron approached our table and greeted us. He set down two glasses of ice water then explained the menu to me. I eventually settled on a delicious-sounding chicken and vegetable meal. Stefano ordered gnocchi—whatever *that* was—as well as two orders of eggplant croquettes and a bottle of wine.

When the waiter left, I asked, "You didn't look very happy when the kitchen staff were saying hello to you."

Stefano's glass hovered at his lips. "It was not a genuine hello."

"So why don't you just tell them to be for real?"

He tilted his head to the side, his brow scrunching, then he nodded. "I cannot tell them to 'be for real,' Claudia. Else, I will never hear the end of it from my parents. All these… centuries-old formalities are just that—centuries old."

"So, what you're trying to say is that they're acting differently because you have money, right?"

"Money has little to do with it. There are just some… politics I don't agree with."

I frowned. "I see." *What could the political structure be like in a seemingly perfect utopia like this?*

The waiter returned—thank goodness—with the wine and croquettes. The darkness in Stefano's face lifted as the waiter set down the plate with a mountain of odd little fried things between us then poured two glasses of a sparkling red wine. After the waiter left, Stefano lifted his glass and looked at me expectantly.

Enthralled by his gaze, I absently lifted my glass and took a small sip. I soon returned to reality. The wine was sweet and slightly fruity with just enough alcohol to give it a little kick. "This is amazing. What is it?"

"It's called Trevisani d'Annata. Made from my own family's vineyard." He sipped at his glass modestly.

Of course his family would own a vineyard. I wondered if he would bleed gold if I pricked his finger. The smell of something fried and delicious drove my attention to the center of the table. I studied the croquettes, which reminded me of hushpuppies, sitting next to a small cup of something that looked like mayonnaise.

Stefano cocked his head. "Try one?"

"Well… okay. They do look good." I selected the smallest one from the bunch. It was hot, but not too hot to touch.

The corner of his mouth tugged into a small smile. "Dip it in the aioli, first, *bella*."

I did so and took a small bite. The fried breaded exterior gave it a slight crunch, then the soft chewy inside melted on my tongue. The garlic aioli mixed with the eggplant and spices was a perfect, mouth-watering combination that had me gobbling up the rest in one bite. "Wow! These are amazing. No wonder you're addicted to them."

Stefano laughed as he plucked a croquette from the top of the heap. He drenched the thing in dip and chomped on it.

"So how long have you been a deejay?" I asked.

"Since college, so I would say about four years or so." He popped another croquette into his mouth.

"You like it?"

He reached for another one, stopped, and looked at me. "I *love* it. It is my escape. Music is one of the most important things in my life. And to be able to share it with others? There is no greater feeling."

I smiled, recalling him saying similar things about music back in high school. "Are you always at that club in Alta Rosa?"

"I am everywhere. Depends on when and where I am needed. But Alta Rosa is where a lot of my gigs come from."

"Is it 'cause it's the capital? Where most of the tourists hang out?"

"No, because my family owns most of the clubs there."

Why am I not surprised? "I see. Well, you're pretty good at what you do. I couldn't stop rocking to those beats last night."

He grinned. "*Grazie.* I want my music to bring happiness to everyone."

I swiped another croquette. There were only a few left on the plate now, thanks to Stefano's seemingly endless craving.

The waiter returned with our main courses. The plate of chicken and vegetables he set in front of me looked absolutely divine, all the way down to the rosemary garnish. Meanwhile, Stefano salivated over his bowl of mini-dumplings. As he picked up his spoon, I heard a faint vibration under the table. Frowning, Stefano set down his spoon, grumbled, and dug his phone out of his pocket. Without even looking at the screen, he shut it off and set it facedown on the table.

"Are you sure you didn't want to answer that?" I asked.

"Positive." He picked up his spoon again.

"But what if it was important?"

He let out a soft laugh. "There's nothing more important to me right now than this gnocchi." He emphasized the point by shoveling a spoonful of mini-dumplings into his mouth.

I laughed and dug into my own meal. Like the croquettes, everything was savory and seasoned perfectly. I would never have thought I would find something I liked almost as much as Mama's down-home Southern cooking.

We enjoyed our meals, with the sounds of the fountain's trickling water providing a relaxing vibe.

The waiter returned shortly after we finished, his face devoid of color. His gaze darted between us before settling on Stefano. "Ah… Y-Your Grace, you are needed inside."

Stefano arched an eyebrow. "Tell whoever it is that I am busy and do not have time to talk."

The waiter gulped. "Ah, b-but—"

Stefano's face darkened. "I said I am busy. Now, *vattene da qui!*"

I moistened my lips and watched the waiter scramble back inside. "What was that all about?"

Stefano downed the last of the wine from his glass then sighed deeply. "I do not know. I just wanted to enjoy some time alone, away from the stresses of life, and have dinner with you like couples do."

I widened my eyes. *Couples? He thinks we're a couple?* "Whoa, wait a minute. I thought we were just having dinner."

He smiled apologetically. "*Scusa,* Claudia. I did not mean it the way it sounded."

Or did he? I pursed my lips.

He opened his mouth, but something suddenly made his face pale, just as the waiter's had been. His widened eyes focused on something behind me. Cursing under his breath, he shot up from his chair.

I looked over my shoulder. The waiter had returned, walking alongside a tall slender woman in a long, form-fitting dark-green cocktail dress. The lights strung from above softened her seemingly flawless, alabaster skin. Curly auburn hair spilled over her shoulders and down her back. Glittering diamond-like gems adorned her ears.

She looked as though she could have been on the cover of *Vogue*. Something bad churned in my gut. It felt like sadness. Jealousy. Envy. I knew I wouldn't be able to control this mix of emotions if I stared at her any longer.

"Mother!" Stefano said breathlessly. His body was tensed, and he looked as though he'd just been caught with his hand in the cookie jar.

Mother? This woman is his mother? My jaw dropped. She looked no older than thirty. And Stefano had to have been no older than twenty-four. Something wasn't right.

The woman stopped before our table and crossed her arms. Her hazel eyes narrowed, and her lips puckered into a tiny red dot as she acknowledged me. Her gaze could have burned a hole in the wall.

Stefano scooted around the table and faced his mother, exasperated. A heated discussion in Italian ensued. Her foot tapping repeatedly, his mother occasionally sneered in my direction as she responded to Stefano. Finally, after several minutes arguing, the veins in Stefano's neck became visible, and he took several breaths, perhaps trying to keep his cool. He gestured to me as he asked his mother something, and I heard my name among the string of Italian phrases. Her perfect face reddened, and she uttered a sharp response through clenched teeth. Finally, she spun on her heel and stormed back inside.

Stefano exhaled, and his shoulders slumped. He turned back to me, his eyes filled with a mix of emotions. "*Scusa*, Claudia. You did not need to see that…"

I stood and approached him. I took his hand in mine and looked at him apologetically. "It's okay. I'm not sure what that conversation was about, but I guess it's safe to assume that you two don't see eye to eye on some things. I understand how hard it is to deal with certain family members." Thoughts of my evil Aunt Jolinda suddenly sprung to mind. That lady always had something negative to say to me. Whether it was about my hair, my clothes, or my passion for art, it didn't matter. That woman didn't have a positive bone in her frail, senile body.

Stefano looked at me carefully then down to our hands. I followed his gaze and suddenly let go. But he took my hand again and rubbed it gently. A small smile crept to his lips. "Shall I take you back to the lodge?"

A brief shiver ran through me like an electric current from my fingertips. I glanced from my hands to him. "O-Okay."

We returned to the waiting car, thankfully, without encountering Stefano's mother again. We rode in silence for what seemed like forever. I could make out Stefano's scowl as the passing streetlights and headlights slid across his face.

"Hey, thanks for dinner," I said, trying to lighten the mood. "It was really nice."

His scowl lifted slightly. "I am glad you enjoyed yourself. I apologize that the night had to end so abruptly."

"It's okay. It happens. We should do dinner again sometime." *Oh geez. What am I saying?*

He smiled at me and nodded. "Sì. I would like that very much."

It was ten at night when we pulled up to the lodge. Stefano helped me out and walked me to the front door. Standing on the steps, we looked at each other. Stefano took my hands in his and looked at them. My heart suddenly started beating faster. His fingers were soft and warm, and I didn't want him to let go.

"*Grazie*, Claudia, for allowing me the honor for tonight." He brought the top of my hands to his lips and kissed them gently.

I felt my cheeks get hot. *Wow, and here I thought that only happened in the movies.* I wished he would do that again.

He finally let go of my hands, much to my disappointment. "May we do something tomorrow?"

This is just a random holiday fling, right? It didn't have to be anything serious, so why was I feeling so worked up over it? *What the hey. Time to live a little and make Trina more jealous.* "Sure."

He inclined his head. "*Ottimo.* I will call you tomorrow, and we can arrange something, okay?"

"Sounds good." I reached for the door handle. "Goodnight, Stefano," I said, realizing just how bittersweet my voice sounded.

His smile faltered. He turned his back to me, but looked at me from over his shoulder. "*Arrivederci,* Claudia."

I remained on the steps of the lodge, staring longingly at the sedan's taillights until they were out of sight.

CHAPTER 5

I HADN'T EXPECTED TO SLEEP IN SO LATE THE next morning. But I'd slept so well! I couldn't stop dreaming of my dinner with Stefano, that beautiful restaurant, that awesome food and wine... then his beautiful but scary mother, who caused me to finally wake up. Groaning, I lay in bed, staring up at the wooden ceiling, wondering what Stefano was up to right then.

I could hear Trina's voice already, telling me to snag him before he got away.

No. I was on vacation, so it was best not to get too attached to the man. *Oh, but what a man he is!*

I rubbed the top of my hand with my thumb, remembering that lovely kiss. I took a deep breath— then another. Being so obsessed over a man was freaking me out just a bit.

The pain on the bottoms of my feet was lessening, and I was starting to feel a little more confident in my steps as I walked. After I'd gotten dressed and grabbed a cappuccino, I headed down to the lake with my art supplies. I needed to concentrate on sketching for at least the next few hours, and not Stefano. Or croquettes. *Those were some good croquettes...*

The tourists were out in full force again, enjoying the mild summer weather. I chose a spot underneath a large shade tree, resting my back against the trunk. I gazed out at the colorful scenery and noted the bluish-purple mountains in the distance. *What a sight. And what a perfect composition.*

I flipped open to a blank page and let my pencils do the work. I was lost in my own world, capturing the true essence of nature, when my hip vibrated, jolting me out of my creative trance. I fumbled for my phone in my pocket and yanked it out, ready to curse whoever it was interrupting me.

Stefano's number flashed on the screen, and the annoyance immediately ebbed. I cleared my throat and answered politely, "Hello?"

"*Buongiorno*, Claudia," Stefano responded in that tantalizing accent.

I took a deep breath. "Uh, h-hi, Stefano."

"I hope I am not disturbing you."

"Oh, no. I was just finishing up another sketch."

"*Bene.* Then perhaps… you may be willing to join me for dinner at my place?"

I froze. At *his place*? An eerie feeling struck the back of my mind. "Uh… I don't know about that…"

After a brief moment of awkward silence, Stefano sighed. "I… I will confess, Claudia. I am inviting you over because… my mother wants to meet you…"

I blinked. "Y-Your mother?"

"Sì. I told her about you, and she is curious."

I swallowed, not liking at all where the conversation was headed. "She looked ready to chew my head off when she saw me."

"Only because she did not know who you were."

"What did you tell her?"

"I told her…" He took a deep breath. "I told her that you were a beautiful American girl that I remembered and liked from high school. That you had the prettiest feet. And you enjoyed eggplant croquettes." He chuckled.

I couldn't help but chuckle, too. But then his words suddenly hit me like bricks. *So he really* did *have a crush on me back then.* "Why would you say that to your mother?"

"Because she would not stop asking who the mysterious girl was with me. And I am not going to lie to her about my feelings for a girl I like. So would you come over and have dinner with me, *per favore?*"

I actually felt sorry for him. He seemed to have the entire world in his grasp, and yet he couldn't even handle his own mother. "All right. Fine. But just one question."

"Sì?"

"How old is your mother?"

There was a slight pause. "Um, forty-eight, why?"

My jaw dropped. "Forty-*eight?* Seriously? She doesn't look a day past thirty!"

"I know. And she likes it that way. Honestly, I cannot stand it."

I opened my mouth, about to ask him what he meant by that, when he continued.

"I will be at the lodge to fetch you shortly."

"All right. I'll be sure to wear my best dress."

Another pause. "Okay..." he said, his voice full of doubt.

Before I could say anything more, Stefano ended the call, and I was left wondering what that good-looking Bellacignan was up to.

Later that afternoon, I lingered in the lobby, wearing a purple strapless, knee-length dress and matching purple heels. I'd brought three special dresses for my four-week trip, with the sole intention of wearing them to the clubs. I read some of the new flyers on the bulletin board, browsed the gift shop, and finally plopped down on the couch. One could easily fall asleep on the super-comfortable cushions.

Suddenly, the front door swung open, and all time stopped. Stefano was decked out in a light-grey dress shirt and black pants. He immediately spotted me and smiled that charming smile. Wisps of his short, curly black hair grazed just above his left eye and down the side of his cheek. As he approached me, the scent of his sandalwood cologne became stronger. I inhaled deeply and closed my eyes, recalling that same scent when he'd held me close the other night.

A few of the female tourists acknowledged Stefano with curiosity and admiration. But Stefano paid them no mind, or maybe he just didn't see them. No, I believed he was ignoring them. He walked right past a well-endowed, bikini-clad blonde who eyed him up and down as if he were dessert.

Stefano stopped in front of me and held out his hand. "Need some help?"

I tried to move, but the cushions swallowed me like quicksand. Blushing, I reached for his hand. His grip tightened, and he effortlessly pulled me onto my feet. I lowered my head, mortified that he'd had to save me from a couch.

He tilted my chin up, and I couldn't look anywhere else but at him. "You look *bellissima,* Claudia, but…"

But? Is there something on my face? A stain on my dress? "But…?"

He opened his mouth to reply then took one look at the people staring at us and gently guided me to the door. "Let us talk outside."

Feeling the many eyes on us, I nodded. Outside, Vittorio was standing next to the sedan, texting on his phone. He looked up briefly, spotted us, and gave us a small salute before returning to his phone.

Stefano took my hand and kissed the top. He looked at me intently, not releasing my hand. "I did not mean to upset or offend you, Claudia. I really do love the dress, but…" He averted his gaze as if lost in thought before returning his attention to me. "My mother is very… old-fashioned. She considers the color purple to be bad luck. Moreover, your dress is way too short."

Pulling my hand away from his, I lifted an eyebrow. "Too short? Are you kidding me? The hem is almost past my knees!" I pressed the hem to my knee to emphasize the point.

Stefano shook his head. "Believe me, *bella*, I think your dress looks *fantastico*. But my mother—"

"Sounds like my crazy aunt who never has anything good to say about what I wear," I finished with a frown. "If shirt sleeves are rolled up, she'll complain, saying too much of my arm is showing. If I wear sandals, she'll complain, saying my feet and ankles are too exposed. Heaven forbid I wear a pair of cargo shorts. She'll most likely have a heart attack." I smirked at that last tempting thought.

Stefano simply looked at me, dumbfounded. "Thankfully, my mother is not that extreme. But as you are the guest of honor—and a foreign one, at that—she will be especially critical of your attire."

"Gee, thanks. You know, you could've said something before."

"*Scusa...*"

"Well, all my dresses are short like this. I mean, come on—it's summer. I need to stay cool. It's too hot to be covering my legs."

"Sì. I completely understand. But for tonight, will you be able to appease my mother's wishes for just a few hours?"

I grunted and shrugged. "I'm not going to buy a brand-new dress for this."

He smiled. "Don't worry. You won't." He took my hand again and led me to the car.

"Wait... no." I snatched my hand away. "You're not going to buy me a dress, either."

Stefano said nothing. Vittorio quickly put his phone away and opened the door for us.

"I mean it, Stefano," I said, not getting in.

Smiling, Stefano shook his head. "Okay. I will not buy you a dress. I promise." He put his right hand over his heart and held up his left.

I looked at him skeptically. "What about your mother, then? I don't want her yelling at me for dressing like this."

"She will not. I will make certain of it." Stefano nodded firmly.

I looked to Vittorio for confirmation. "Well, Vittorio? What do *you* have to say about this?"

Vittorio cleared his throat as he scratched the back of his head. "Ah, His Grace is always true to his word, Signorina Gray."

Somehow, I still didn't find that very reassuring.

The silence after we'd left the lodge seemed to stretch for an eternity. My stomach churned with a constant bad feeling. *Maybe this was a bad idea after all.* But something about Stefano got me all tongue-tied and indecisive.

"Are you okay, Claudia?" Stefano asked, placing his hand over mine.

I stared at our hands, and my mind drifted again. Would meeting his family really be so bad? We weren't exactly complete strangers. Stefano was a perfect gentleman, which was more than I could say about some of the guys I'd met back home during my college years. Men like Stefano were seemingly rare these days.

I finally looked at him and said, "Yeah, I'm fine. Just wondering what to say to your mom."

He smiled. "Just be yourself. However... do address her as 'Your Grace.'"

"Of course. Titles of the rich and famous, and all that."

He gave a slight smile.

The car stopped. Looking out the window, I noticed we were parked along the curb in front of a fancy department store. Vittorio opened the back door.

"Why are we here?" I asked.

Stefano looked at me apologetically. "Ah... since you are meeting my mother, it is considered polite in Bellacignan customs for a foreigner to bring a small gift for the host family." He extended his hand to help me out of the car. "Come, Claudia. We shall not be long."

I pursed my lips and got out reluctantly. *A gift. Of course.* First impressions were everything, after all. Stefano guided me through the revolving mahogany door. The door alone told me that anything in the store required very deep pockets. My suspicions were confirmed when we stood in the grand entrance of a luxurious department store. Black-tile flooring was polished to a shine, giant chandeliers hung from high, design-inlaid ceilings, and red-velvet curtains draped high-arched display windows that looked out onto the city's main street. Abstract paintings of all shapes, sizes, and mediums hung from the ivory-colored walls. Expensive-looking vases, stone columns, and statues decorated the place with an old-Renaissance vibe. The air was crisp and bathed in the scents of new leather and perfumes.

I noticed a cute little blue clutch purse in a display case—with a six-figure price... *Why are we here again?*

Customers, mostly older women, wandered about the store dressed in designer pants, shoes, and blouses, their hair done in designer styles, and carrying designer purses. Most walked past me, paying me no mind. Others were too preoccupied with their diamond-studded cellphones at their ears to notice me. *Uncomfortable* didn't begin to describe how I felt, standing amid so much money in once place. What was Stefano thinking to bring me to a place like this?

Stefano released my hand. "I will be right back. Why don't you have a look around?"

I lifted an eyebrow. *For what? My entire life savings isn't even enough to cover a single button on one of those blouses.* "Uh... sure."

He disappeared down a clothes aisle, leaving me standing very still in front of a rack of purses that I dared not touch. I wondered if I would be charged for breathing in here, too. But then a dress in the distance caught my eye—a shimmering, royal-blue evening gown, truly the most beautiful dress I'd ever laid eyes on. I walked—very slowly and very carefully—toward the graceful mannequin wearing the strapless, backless, floor-length gown. I could imagine myself wearing that—maybe in my dreams.

I looked around for a price tag but found none. I guessed that meant it took way too many zeroes for the tiny tag to hold. I could at least take a picture and fantasize about it, right? Smiling, I took out my cell phone and snapped the perfect picture.

"You like that dress?"

I jumped, hearing Stefano's voice directly behind me, and nearly dropped my phone. "Oh! Uh, yeah, it's beautiful."

The corners of Stefano's eyes wrinkled as his smile grew. Tucked underneath his arm was a small box wrapped in powder-blue-colored paper. "Sì. I think you would look *bellissima*." He paused. "Wait here, *un momento*."

He walked off again and caught up with a young, beautiful blonde in a dark-blue knee-length skirt and blouse. She wore a pair of pumps spiked so high, I was amazed by her impeccable balance. She cast a perfect smile at Stefano and regarded him with adorable green eyes. Something about her reminded me of him. Maybe those were the types of girls he liked. He seemed very comfortable around her, and the sight made something twinge in my gut.

I looked around for the exit, but had no idea where I was in this gigantic maze of a store, so I just picked a direction and started walking. *What am I doing? I can't possibly be feeling like some helpless jealous fool.*

I walked with firmer steps. *I'm not getting attached to this man. Yet I'm about to meet his mother. Why did we come to this store again?* My mind continued racing as I frantically looked for the exit, where Vittorio would hopefully be waiting.

"Claudia!" The sound of Stefano's footsteps approached.

I sucked in a breath and halted. I looked over my shoulder.

"Claudia, are you okay? You left so quickly..." Stefano said, his brow pinched.

I pursed my lips. "May we please go, now?"

Stefano continued looking at me oddly, then he nodded. "Of course." He reached for my hand. "But Eileen just needed to get your measurements first."

I arched an eyebrow. "Eileen? Measurements?"

"Hello," the blonde said, waving at me as she came up from behind him.

The feeling in my gut returned. I looked at Stefano. "Who is this?"

Stefano smiled. "This is my cousin, Eileen. She is the store owner. She needed to get your measurements for the blue dress."

"It will not take long, Signorina Claudia," Eileen finished with a polite smile.

I felt as though a horse had just kicked me in the face. *Cousin?* I cleared my throat. "Uh… wait. Stefano, I thought you promised you wouldn't buy me a dress?"

His smile remained. "I did, and I am not."

"It is a gift from me, signorina," Eileen said. "A thank-you gift for bringing such happiness to Stefano."

"Happiness? Huh?" I looked back and forth between them. My gaze then remained on Stefano. "What is she talking about?"

Before he could answer, Eileen escorted me away, toward the changing room. "Stefano has been quite unhappy until recently. I had been worried for him. But then he told me so much about you, and I could hear the happiness in his voice. Thank you, Claudia, for helping him."

I looked over my shoulder at Stefano, who currently had his phone to his ear. I looked back at his cousin. "Helping him with what? I didn't do anything."

"I think you have done more than you know."

She got me all measured up, retrieved the dress from the mannequin, and did a quick alteration. Afterward, she handed me the dress, along with a matching pair of shoes with three-inch heels. I stood before the dressing room mirror, dress in hand, wondering if all of this was still a dream.

"Please come out when you are finished getting dressed, so that I can check for any final adjustments," Eileen called from the other side of the door.

It took several minutes, but finally, I stepped out of my old dress and shoes and into the gown of my dreams.

It fit perfectly. Eileen's alteration skills were top-notch. I ran my fingers along the light material, which was softer than silk. The shoes fit comfortably, like pillows on my feet, despite having three-inch heels.

I'd just entered a fairy tale. There was no way I could accept something so extravagant as a gift. I stepped out of the dressing room and discovered Eileen and Stefano waiting. Stefano's eyes bugged out.

Eileen clapped her hands. "*Bellissima*! It fits you perfectly!"

I quirked a shy smile, trying to be modest. Stefano stood like a statue, his eyes still wide and his mouth hanging open. Eileen playfully slapped him on the back, startling him from his trance.

"Is he okay?" I asked.

She nodded and winked at me. "He is fine. This is *the* dress, Claudia. You have him mesmerized."

I chuckled lightly and looked at Stefano, who still seemed at a loss of words. Then I sighed and looked back at Eileen. "I can't accept all this for free. I mean..."

Eileen cocked an eyebrow and put her hands on her hips. "And why not? It is my store. I make the decisions around here. And I have decided that you are the perfect candidate for that dress and those shoes."

I opened my mouth to argue, but then her other eyebrow rose, so I said instead, "Thank you."

Her face softened once more, and she led us out of the store. Vittorio was on his phone again, leaned up against the hood, but when he saw us, he promptly ended the call and rushed to open the back door.

As we drove off, Eileen waved from the shop's entrance, a satisfied smile on her face. We rode on in silence, as Stefano kept casting sideways glances at me, probably trying not to look so obvious, but he was doing a terrible job.

It was an awkward situation, and I could hear Trina's voice in my head say, "Girl, if that's all it took to make him tongue-tied, you should've done that sooner!"

CHAPTER 6

WE PULLED THROUGH AN EXQUISITE WROUGHT-iron gate. Small white lights decorated the top, mimicking little stars twinkling in the night. I sucked in a breath and peered through the windshield as we approached a massive villa that looked like something straight out of Renaissance Italy. Trees lined the long cobblestone driveway the sedan crept along, and ivy, flowers, and other flora decorated the stone walls of the mansion's exterior. *I thought places like this only existed in home-improvement magazines and TV shows. And Stefano's mother lives here?*

We pulled up to the grand entrance, and I plastered my face to the window like an excited toddler. My heart suddenly started pounding.

"Claudia…"

I snapped out of my thoughts. Stefano was already out of the car and had extended his hand to me. I looked at his hand, dumbfounded, then slowly reached for it. Our fingers touched, and my hand shook from the initial contact, but he grabbed it quickly.

Stefano grinned, and all my nervousness seemed to melt away. "Come. My mother awaits us."

I gulped and got out the car. He let go of my hand and placed his at the small of my back. I flinched in surprise. He'd never touched me there before. But it felt nice. *Warm.*

I suddenly realized I hadn't worn any makeup for the occasion. *Geez. What's wrong with me to forget to wear makeup?*

Vittorio opened the door—ornate, oak doors that were designed with various intricate engravings that probably cost more than a lottery's earning just for one single cut.

Holding my breath, I followed Stefano inside. My shoes clacked against the polished, blue-stone marble floors. Cool refreshing air hit my skin, and I exhaled in awe at the immaculate interior. A grand staircase spiraled upward to the floors above. Royal-blue silk drapes covered the giant floor-to-ceiling windows, but a small break in the curtains allowed a sliver of light from the rising moon to peek through. The toned-down lights from the vintage wall sconces and the more modern inset track lights above created a warm atmosphere.

I looked back at the entrance, where Stefano and Vittorio stood speaking in hushed tones. Vittorio rushed down one of the grand halls. Moments later, a well-dressed man and woman approached us. I recognized the man as Filippo, the limo driver. I smiled and waved to him, and he cast a nervous smile back before bowing his head.

"*Buonasera*, Signorina Claudia," Filippo said hastily. His gaze bounced to Stefano.

Stefano met his gaze, and he raised an eyebrow expectantly. Filippo lowered his head, approached Stefano slowly, and muttered something in his ear. Stefano's face grew dark, and he nodded. Afterward, Filippo rushed out of sight.

Stefano turned to me. "*Scusa*, Claudia. But I need to take care of something." He motioned to the woman. "Gemma, here, is one of the housekeepers. Let her know if you have any questions."

The older woman acknowledged me with a polite and warm grandmotherly smile.

Without another word, Stefano followed Filippo down the hall.

I looked at Gemma in silence, too overwhelmed to ask her anything.

Small creases on her face appeared as her smile grew. She must've sensed my fluster. "Come, signorina. You probably want to get freshened up before dinner," she said in a soft, sweet tone.

She led me through the grand hall then down another passage with closed-off rooms. I could smell chicken, fish, and spices nearby. My mouth watered. We stopped in front of an oak door with a simple design of a laurel near the top. She turned the gold knob, and the door opened to a massive, dimly lit marble bathroom twice the size of my bedroom. A giant Jacuzzi sat in one corner, and a walk-in shower as big as my entire bathroom filled the other. The large countertop held two sinks, their metal faucets shining like new.

I stood in the doorway, gawking like an idiot at the most beautiful bathroom I'd ever seen. An elite interior decorator from a home-improvement TV show could never top something like this.

"Signorina, dinner starts in ten *minuti*. I shall fetch you shortly," Gemma said, as if not noticing my ogling. She pushed me gently into the bathroom and closed the door behind me.

I looked over my shoulder at the closed door and sighed. *I'm here. In Stefano's house—no,* castle. I couldn't begin to fathom how much money was invested in just the soft, fur bath mat alone that I was currently standing on.

I quickly got off it, fearing I would get slapped with a "loitering on the bath mat" bill. I didn't dare touch a single thing in there, much less use the toilet or wash my hands. *This is ridiculous. I should at least be able to wash my hands.* I extended a shaky hand toward one of the faucets and gently turned it on as if it were made of glass. Water trickled out, then the flow got stronger. The soap dispenser, which was a small metal box that matched the faucet, sat conveniently next to it. I washed my hands with the rose-scented soap and dried them on a hand towel folded neatly between the two sinks. I carefully refolded the towel, smoothed it, and returned it to its rightful place.

I checked my face, my hair... and my dress, which was truly fit for royalty. *I guess tonight I'll be Cinderella for a few hours.* No one back home would believe me if I told them of my adventures. Trina would be especially jealous.

There was a small knock at the door. "Signorina Claudia. Are you ready?"

I stopped in mid-twirl of admiring my dress, wondering how much time had passed. I cleared my throat and headed to the door. "Uh, yes, sure." I opened it a crack, and Gemma's warm smile welcomed me again.

"Come, then." She gestured with a small tilt of her head.

I followed her through the house, admiring more exquisite rooms, stone statues, and high ceilings displaying a mural similar to the famous one in the Sistine Chapel. The dining room table seated at least twenty. Only one end of the ivory-clothed table was set, however. Four placements. *Four?*

It must've been a mistake. It was supposed to be me, Stefano, and his mother, right?

Gemma guided me to a seat. I wondered where Stefano was. Once I was situated, Gemma inclined her head and started backing away to another room, then disappeared around the corner.

I looked at my table setting. The shiny porcelain dishes were out of this world. Trimmed with gold and floral designs, they were absolutely gorgeous. Mama's special china had nothing on this stuff. The red cloth napkin, folded in a neat *origami*-looking design, housed the matching gold utensils. The drinkware appeared to be made of pure crystal. I wouldn't have been surprised if it was.

There was a setting at the head of the table and two opposite me, but none beside me. I sat there, my mind swimming about where Stefano might sit— probably beside his mother, who would be sitting at the head. And I would be sitting on this side of the table all alone, with their eyes constantly on me. I figured the fourth person was going to sit next to Stefano.

A door opened farther down the hall. A young woman appeared, dressed in a long silver gown. She had short brown hair, creamy skin, and sapphire-blue eyes. She was accompanied by another housekeeper dressed similarly to Gemma. As the woman took her seat across from me, I raised my eyebrows at her. She looked like a supermodel with her perfectly high cheekbones and full lips.

"Hello," I said, my voice echoing in the great hall.

"*Buonasera.*" She inclined her head.

"I don't believe we've met…"

"Oh, *scusi*. I am Mirella Soriano. Pleased to meet you, signorina…"

"Claudia. Gray." My throat tightened. "You're here for dinner, too?"

She bit her bottom lip and averted her gaze. "Ah, sì. But I had no idea that—" She paused and looked up at the sound of another door opening. She suddenly stood from her chair.

I furrowed my brow and looked to where she was temporarily gawking. Stefano's mother entered, dressed in a luxurious evening gown less magnificent than the one she'd been wearing at the restaurant. She eyed the two of us at the table, her gaze lingering on me a little longer, and stood behind her chair. Her lips pursed, and her eyes narrowed as she continued staring at me with a disgusted look.

"Signorina, please stand..." Gemma suddenly whispered from behind me.

I flinched. *Where did she come from? That old lady is stealthier than a ninja.* Sucking in a breath, I slowly stood. I noticed Mirella had her head lowered, so I did the same, though I watched Stefano's mother from the corner of my eye.

Stefano's mother took a seat, and Mirella followed suit. I was the last to sit.

His mother scowled at Gemma and muttered something sharply in Italian. Gemma lowered her head and replied. Then she backed away slowly and headed for the exit. But she stopped in her tracks as Stefano stood there, his face redder than the cloth napkins. He stormed into the dining room and stood beside my chair. He looked over the placements, and his face grew darker.

"Mother, what is this?" he demanded.

His mother raised her eyebrows and replied in Italian. Then she gestured to the empty seat beside Mirella.

"Fine." He rounded the table, grabbed his table setting, and carried it over to a place next to me. "And I would appreciate it if Claudia was a part of our conversations."

His mother gaped, and her face reddened. "Stefano! Where are your manners?"

"They are still here. There was an obvious mistake in the placement." He sat down beside me.

His mother's eyes grew wide. "Mirella wanted to meet you. I think she is a nice young lady."

I looked over to Mirella, who frowned at the two of us. Like Stefano, she was probably born into money. Of course his mother would have a problem with a foreign commoner like me being around her son. He deserved a girl with a lifestyle similar to his. Mirella was someone his mother approved of. My throat tightened a little more. *Why am I really here?*

Stefano looked at Mirella apologetically. "*Scusa* for the miscommunication."

Mirella shook her head slowly. "It is all right, Your Grace. Really."

"If you do not wish to stay for dinner, I can have Vittorio take you home," Stefano said.

His mother barked something in Italian and slapped her hand on the table.

Mirella and I jumped, but Stefano remained calm. He flicked his gaze at his mother. "Mother, you set me up, and I find it disgraceful." He focused on Mirella again. "Now, would you like Vittorio to take you home?"

Mirella looked at him, then at me, and frowned. She lowered her head and nodded once.

84

Stefano took out his phone, sent a quick text, then put it away. "He will fetch you shortly."

His mother fumed. "How dare you, Stefano! Mirella is a respectable young lady."

Mirella looked as if she wanted to say something, but held her tongue.

Before Stefano could retort, the servants came out carrying trays of covered dishes. Each one set a plate in front of us. A servant uncovered mine, revealing a steaming bowl of tomato-based soup with pasta, vegetables, and small white beans. Another servant poured red wine into each of the crystalline glasses. Though everything looked and smelled divine, my appetite was shot. I spotted Stefano's fists clenching and unclenching under the table. He scowled at his food.

His mother cleared her throat. "Let us enjoy dinner." She picked up her spoon and nodded to the rest of us.

Stefano hesitated then grabbed his spoon and dunked it into his soup. He took a forceful bite, as if it were the most disgusting thing he'd ever tasted. Mirella followed his lead, eating more daintily—as if she were doing it out of sheer obligation.

Then it was my turn. While I wasn't hungry, I was still curious about how a home-cooked meal tasted here. So I indulged, taking a hefty bite of the hot soup. It tasted as good as it smelled. The pasta and broth melted on my tongue, invigorating my appetite. I thought I could polish it off.

Vittorio entered the dining room and announced his presence with a bow. I made out Mirella's name among the Italian words.

Mirella dabbed her mouth with a napkin and stood quietly. She inclined her head at us. "*Grazie* for the lovely dinner, Your Graces." She glanced at me. "It was a pleasure meeting you, Signorina Gray." Then she disappeared down the hall with Vittorio.

With just me, Stefano, and his mother left, the awkward silence that followed made my skin prickle. I debated whether or not to eat more of the delicious soup, but since Stefano was not, I willed my hand to remain at my side.

His mother regarded me with a frown then spoke sharp, Italian phrases to Stefano.

Stefano lifted his head, his eyes piercing the woman like daggers. "Mother, I will not hide our conversations from Claudia any longer. And there was nothing wrong with Mirella. She obviously did not want to be here. I am disappointed in you for lying to me."

I watched as Gemma quietly came in and cleared away Mirella's place setting.

Stefano's mother let out a sharp laugh. "I did not lie to you, Stefano. I really did want to meet Signorina Gray."

"For what reason?" Stefano narrowed his eyes. "To make her feel uncomfortable like she is probably feeling now?" His jaw clenched. He cast a glance at me then looked back at his mother.

Oh, he had no *idea…*

She shook her head and narrowed her eyes slightly. "No. I wanted to *talk* to her."

"Talk to her about what?" he asked cautiously.

Gemma moved around my side of the table and refilled Stefano's wine glass.

I cleared my throat, unable to hear or see any more of their bickering. I stood up quickly. "I'm sorry, but I should probably leave. I might be able to catch Vittorio before he leaves with Mirella."

A small gasp came from Gemma. Standing so close to me, she gave me a worried look. Then her gaze shifted to Stefano and his mother. "Signorina Gray, it is impolite to dismiss yourself before the duchess…" she whispered to me while she topped off my wine glass, though I'd only taken a few sips.

I blinked. "Wait… what? Duchess?" I pointed to Stefano's mother as I said to Gemma, "You mean she's not just another simple noble or foreign celebrity? She's *royalty?*"

Both Stefano and his mother looked at me in horror. Then they eyed Gemma, who rushed out the room, uttering a series of apologies.

When the servant was gone, Stefano stood and reached for my hand. "Claudia..."

"You mean she does not even *know* who *I* am? Who *you* are?" The duchess seethed and pointed a perfectly manicured, red-nail-polished fingertip at me.

I felt a lump in my throat. The servants started to come out with the main course dishes, but they stopped in their tracks when they noticed the commotion in the dining room. They immediately retreated to the kitchen without a word.

Stefano cast his mother a glare then turned back to me. "Claudia, can you—"

"She does not even know!" The duchess stood and slapped her palms on the table again, causing the glassware and utensils to rattle violently.

"Mother!" Stefano said through gritted teeth.

She stormed over to us and stood between Stefano and me. Her face came so close to mine that our noses almost touched. Looking me in the eye, she pursed her lips. "My irresponsible *son*, Stefano Trevisani of the royal Trevisani Family, is the Duke of Cittàcigni!"

My ears burned. *What?*

"Mother, stop!" Stefano put his hand on her shoulder, but she shook it off violently.

"That means, Signorina Gray, it is fruitless for you, a foreigner and a commoner, to have any relationship with him. Cittàcigni thrives on its age-old cultures and traditions."

"Mother, that is enough!"

The voices, the chaos all around me made it harder to process that information. My head pounded as Stefano and his mother continued their arguing. *Duke? Royal Family? Stefano?* A bitter taste formed in my mouth. It was too much. My body convulsed. I dropped to my knees and vomited all over the duchess's sparkling emerald-colored shoes.

CHAPTER 7

I WASN'T SURE HOW LONG I'D BEEN ASLEEP, BUT when I finally opened my eyes, I found myself staring up at an ornate ceiling. *Ugh! I'm still here!* I wished I were dreaming. Streaks of sunlight poured through a nearby window. Light snoring came from one corner of the room. Sitting up in bed, I looked around. Stefano was slumped in a chair, his head lolling to the side.

I drew back the covers and slid out of bed. I wasn't sure what time it was, but I needed to get out of there. Fast. Memories of last night's disaster suddenly flooded my mind.

Stefano's a duke—the *duke! And I made a complete fool of myself in front of him* and *his mother!*

My feet touched the soft, padded floor. A chill ran down my spine and between my legs. I gasped, realizing that I was wearing nothing but a long silk nightgown. My heart pounding, I looked over at Stefano again. Had he undressed me?

Stefano snorted himself awake and lifted his head. He looked in my direction and hopped up from his chair. He swept over to me and took my hand. "Claudia! What are you doing out of bed? You should not be—"

I pulled my hand away. "Why am I here? And where are my clothes? I just want to go back to the lodge…"

He pursed his lips and nodded. "Very well. But please, will you let me explain first?"

"Explain why you led me on?" My heart raced.

Stefano's shoulders slumped. "I did not mean to upset you, Claudia. I do not go around flaunting my title. I am rather dreading such a responsibility, having to fill my late father's shoes."

"*Late* father?" I bit my bottom lip, suddenly feeling about two inches tall.

He nodded solemnly. "Sì. He died of a stroke six years ago. Being a duke is a daunting task, and my mother does not make it any easier for me when she nags."

"You don't seem to have any responsibilities with all the deejaying you do."

"Music calms me. That is why I enjoy deejaying. But believe me, Claudia, as a duke, I have plenty of responsibilities. There are lots of things that go on behind the scenes. Boring things, tedious things. I have to be involved in traditional community affairs that have been outdated for decades now. I would rather our city get with the times and have more events suited for the younger generation, you know? But my mother would not allow such a thing to happen."

I raised my eyebrows. "What does it matter what she thinks? You are the duke."

"She is still the duchess and has the last word until she either deems it fit for me to rule, or until I…" His gaze faltered from mine, and he frowned.

"Until you what?"

He looked back at me, his eyes carrying a small twinkle of hope. "Until I marry."

I made a face. "As in a marriage of convenience? Seriously? That's so… old-fashioned."

He shook his head. "I don't want it to be of convenience. I want to marry a woman whom I love deeply, and I hope that she will love me the same way, too." His eyes remained on me.

"Oh…" I looked away. This conversation had just steered itself into something awkward. "Well, you seem to already have that taken care of."

"What do you mean?"

I made a fleeting gesture. "That girl, Mirella, right? Isn't she the one you'll most likely marry?"

His expression hardened. "Mirella is a girl my mother wants me to marry. But, you, Claudia… you have stolen my heart."

My own heart stopped for a moment when he said those words. "W-What! Are you saying you want to *marry* me? I've only known you for like… a week!"

"I feel like we have known each other for longer than a week. And in some ways, we have."

"High school doesn't count."

He smiled softly. "You have not changed since high school, *bella*."

"We barely talked or saw each other except in class or occasionally at lunch."

"Sì, but I have not forgotten each and every one of those brief moments."

I sighed. His words were sweet, but I couldn't let myself get caught up in him, not when I would be leaving for home in a couple of weeks. "I think it would do well for your country if you married a non-foreigner and non-commoner."

His smile fell and his eyes narrowed. "No. I will not marry someone I do not love. That is a centuries-old tradition that I would rather let remain where it belongs—in the past. Cittàcigni lives in the past under my mother's rule. I live for the future."

I sighed. "I'm sorry, Stefano. I don't want to talk about this anymore. Please take me back to the lodge… and where are my clothes?"

He shook his head. "The dress was so badly soiled, I had it discarded." He nodded toward another corner of the room. "There are some fresh clothes waiting for you there."

Badly soiled? Cringing, I shut my eyes and clapped my hand over my mouth. I didn't know what was worse: the fact that the most beautiful dress I'd ever laid eyes on was forever destroyed or that I'd experienced the most embarrassing moment of my life. "Ugh! I can't believe I—please tell your mother that I'm sorry."

Stefano laughed, and I opened my eyes. "Sorry? It was rather funny, really. I had not laughed so hard in a very long time."

My hand slid from my mouth. "But, Stefano, that was your mother... the *duchess!* I did such a horrible thing."

"It served her right for being so rude to you at dinner." He grinned at me. "You never cease to amaze me, Claudia. You make me laugh and smile no matter how angry or sad I feel. You have given me new life worth living. You have given me strength that I never knew I had."

"I didn't do anything..." I averted my gaze again. "Look, can I please go back to the lodge now?"

He sighed deeply and nodded. "Very well, if you insist. Vittorio will take you back. I have a charity event to prepare for in which I will be the resident deejay, so I will be unable to join you."

"That's okay. I think it's for the best."

"May I call you, at least?"

I bit my bottom lip. His tone made the offer sound more tempting than it should have. What should've just been a simple vacation fling had spiraled out of control. I needed to distance myself from him. Far, far away. "No, please don't. Thank you for your hospitality. I'm sorry it couldn't have been on better terms."

His shoulders slumped again, and he nodded slowly. "Okay... well, I guess I will let you alone to get dressed." He headed for the door, reached for the handle, and looked back at me. "I do like you, Claudia. Ever since high school. I wish we could have spent more time together. There has been no other girl quite like you."

I practically melted inside, but I made a conscious effort not to show it. A relationship with him would never work, not when he has so many responsibilities. We lived in completely different worlds. And he seemed to want something from me that I was not quite ready to commit to. "Thank you, Stefano. Perhaps if the situation would have been a little different, I could say the same for you." I went over to the clothes: a pair of jeans, a light-grey T-shirt, undergarments, and sneakers. But as simple as the garments looked, I noticed the designer label on the tag in the jeans and figured those alone cost about a week's pay.

Stefano gave me one last look, his eyes full of sadness, and walked out the door. I stared at the closed door, frowning, wondering what life might've been like if I were the lucky girl to accept his hand in marriage.

I stared out the rear-passenger window at Stefano standing at the front door as Vittorio drove off. Even through the sedan's heavily tinted windows, Stefano's eyes were still focused on mine, as if he were staring deep into my soul. Vittorio pulled out of the driveway, and Stefano continued to stare, unmoving. I craned my neck then finally peered out the back window to see if he remained there, and sure enough, he did. Finally, once we had gone around a curve, Stefano was out of sight. I somehow had a feeling he was still there, and it made my heart flutter.

It's best that I don't get too attached to him. I pursed my lips and exhaled deeply through my nose. My rational side was right. Stefano and I led two totally different lives. It needed to stay that way.

The ride back to the lodge was silent. But Vittorio occasionally glanced back at me in the rearview mirror. I wondered what was going through his head. I was sure he'd seen and heard what had been going on between Stefano and me. I'd hoped he didn't ask me about it.

As the lodge came into view, I considered a thought. Stefano knew where I was staying, and I suspected he would drop in again, unannounced. *Maybe I should check out of here. Leave Cittàcigni and find a place to stay in Alta Rosa, instead. Yeah.* Stefano would never know. And the less I saw of him, the faster I would get over him.

Staying in a new place in the capital city might do well for my artistic inspiration, too. A little change in scenery would be good for the creative mind.

Vittorio pulled up to the lodge, and I let myself out without waiting for him to get the door. He rushed around the side of the car to meet me, but he was too late. I was already out, and he gave me a defeated look. I smiled apologetically at him. "Thank you for the ride, Vittorio. I appreciate your service."

He tipped his invisible hat at me. "Anytime, signorina. Do take care."

"You, too."

I watched him get back in the car and leave. Then I headed inside and let the woman at the front desk know that I would be checking out early the next morning.

I'd made the right choice by checking out when I did. Before long, I'd found a small, secluded hotel on the outskirts of Alta Rosa, and I'd been staying there for the past week. It was perfect. I'd filled my book with all sorts of sketches, making my portfolio the best it could be in such a short time. There were no distractions on the city's outskirts. And no Stefano.

Stefano… I gritted my teeth. I still hadn't forgotten about that mysterious duke. I'd blocked his number from my phone, and I was determined to get over him one way or another. But unfortunately, I'd seen some DJ Notte flyers posted in the hotel lobby advertising some of his upcoming gigs. Getting over him was proving to be more difficult than I'd anticipated.

Alta Rosa's outskirts were just as pretty and lush as Cittàcigni's: mountains, rolling hills, and colorful flora. It was an artist's dream. *I should've come here instead, then maybe I wouldn't have ever run into Stefano.*

I cursed my thoughts of him and refocused on finishing the shading of my latest sketch—a small olive tree that sat in a decorative pot in my hotel room. It was one of my best sketches yet, and it had taken me no time at all. *I think I'm starting to like drawing trees again. Mr. Ross would be proud.*

The hotel phone on my night table rang, and I jumped in my bed with a start. *Who could be calling me?* I'd only told Trina where I'd be, but it was seven in the morning in Columbia, which meant she was most likely at work by now, so I assumed it had to be the front desk. I reached over and grabbed the receiver.

"H-Hello?" I said.

"*Buongiorno*, Signorina Gray," a man said. "This is the front desk. You have a visitor who wishes to see you."

I furrowed my brow. "Who is it?"

"Ah…" The man paused. "S-Signor Stefano Trevisani…"

My heart stopped. "The Duke of Cittàcigni?"

"Ah… s-sì. I was, ah, instructed to not mention his formal title."

For what reason, I wonder? I pursed my lips. Part of me felt cynical enough to leave him waiting down there for hours in hopes that he would simply give up and leave. How did he know where I was staying? Was he stalking me? *Maybe I should just hear him out one last time. I'll get the answers I need.* I took a deep breath. "Okay, I'll be right down."

I put away my art supplies and went down to the lobby. As I stepped off the elevator, my heart leaped into my throat. Lounging on one of the couches was Stefano, all dressed up in an urban street outfit, as though ready to go to one of his deejay gigs. He had a pair of sunglasses on, as well as a backward hat. He blended right in with the rest of the young crowd, who didn't seem to pay him any mind. Maybe they didn't realize who he was.

Stefano spotted me and hopped up. He swept over to me and extended his arms for a hug, but I didn't advance. He stood there with his arms outstretched for a few moments, then finally, he dropped them. Sighing, his shoulders slumping, he inclined his head and said, "I just want to talk, Claudia. May we go somewhere private?"

I rubbed my chin then remembered the outdoor balcony seating area that overlooked the mountains and a beautiful lake. Hopefully, there was an unoccupied table for two out there.

"Sure. I just need a drink first," I said, gesturing with my head for him to follow.

We stopped at the bar so I could get a cappuccino. The amused look I'd received from the male attendant had me royally confused and annoyed to the point that I made it a priority to ask Stefano about it as soon as possible.

Following the signs to the balcony, we walked up a narrow, spiraling staircase and through a set of double doors. The mild, crisp air welcomed us as we stepped outside. Only a few people occupied the tables and lounge chairs, and Stefano and I managed to snag a tiny table in the corner that had the best view.

Stefano pulled the chair out for me, and I graciously sat. After seating himself, he glanced out at the landscape and smiled. "This is one of the most beautiful places in Bellacigna."

I followed his gaze. Its picture-perfect, cloudless landscape was a project I'd already sketched. "Yes, it's wonderful to draw inspiration from." I took a sip of my drink and stared at its light-brown contents. "You know, I keep getting funny looks every time I order a cappuccino." I looked at him. "What's up with that? Do Bellacignans hate it or something?"

He quirked a smile. "On the contrary, they like it very much. However, many of the natives are of Italian heritage, and as such, they carry some similar customs—like not drinking anything containing milk after eleven in the morning."

I arched an eyebrow. "Why? Are they lactose intolerant or something?"

"No, milk is believed to disrupt digestion, so Bellacignans just do not drink it after meals." He shrugged. "I happen to like milk, actually, though I have grown up only drinking it in the mornings, and it is a habit that has remained with me even now."

I nodded and finished my drink. I couldn't bear having a cappuccino only in the mornings, so I guess I'd just have to ignore the amused looks from the natives. "Okay." I shifted in my seat. "So tell me why you're here and how you found me."

He sighed and traced his finger along the edge of the table. "I called every hotel all over Bellacigna. It took a while. But... I just had to see you and tell you how sorry I am about what happened. I... miss you and..." He moistened his lips with his tongue. "And I think I am in love with you."

I blinked, almost not believing my ears. *Geez, he loves me!* My heart skipped a beat for a second, but then reality took control of my mind. *No, I can't get involved with him.* "Sorry, Stefano, but we can never be. We live in two different worlds. You're a duke, destined for a big responsibility that I don't think I'm ready to be a part of. But I'm sure there are plenty of other girls out there who are."

Stefano's eyes grew dark. "Perhaps, but I would not feel the same way for them like I feel about you."

"You need a girl like Mirella. She's perfect for you, Stefano. Pretty, seems to come from a wealthy family, is a Bellacignan native, and your mother approves of her. What more do you want?"

"She may be all of those things, but I do not want her. I want you."

I sighed. *This is getting us nowhere.*

"I want to change things, Claudia," he continued. "I want Cittàcigni to be a place where people like us can truly feel at home."

I arched an eyebrow. "'People like us'?"

"Young people who know what they want to do in their life but have not quite made it there yet. Aspiring artists and innovators. Not just the well-off and already established. Cittàcigni can be so much more than what it is now, with a little change."

"So why aren't you making it happen?"

He frowned. "My mother. She is so bent on tradition and keeping the old ways, there is no getting through to her. She is technically the ruling duchess until she deems me fit to take her place. But if I were to marry, then she would have no choice but to step down."

"So you *do* want a marriage of convenience!" I fumed.

"No! Of course not! I really do love you, Claudia. I swear, this has nothing to do with the politics. I could think of no better person to be by my side than you."

I crossed my arms. He was sweet on the words, but I wasn't quite buying it. "Why don't you just stand up to your mother? Tell her how you really feel?"

"It is not that easy..."

"What are you talking about? Just tell her what the situation is. Tell her how you feel about Cittàcigni, and what you plan to do to improve it. Stand up to her, Stefano. Be the duke *you* want to be and not what society expects you to be."

"She… still has not gotten over my father's death. She wants me to be like him, the way he ruled with tradition. He was one of my great-uncle, King Gaspare's many siblings. Everyone loved my father. I could never fill his shoes if I even tried."

"So is that also why you've hesitated in confronting your mother?"

He nodded once.

Closing my eyes for a moment, I rubbed my temples as I went over this conversation in my head. I opened my eyes. "I'm sorry, Stefano. I can't—and I won't—marry you. I have a life of my own in America. I'm leaving next Monday."

His face paled, and he sat back in his chair, exhaling. He ran his hand through his hair. "So is that it, then? I will never see you again?"

"Not like this. It's for the best, Stefano."

"What will you be doing with your life in America?"

"Looking for a job. Hopefully, a teaching job. Or maybe working at an art production company. I've just about finished my portfolio, and I'm pretty happy with it."

He tilted his head, and his brow pinched in curiosity. "So you have not secured a job yet?"

I shook my head. "Not yet, but I have about six months' worth of savings in the meantime." I emphasized that point, in hopes that Stefano would take the hint and not spend more money on me.

Stefano nodded. "Well, then. You have made your decision. But may I ask a final request?"

I raised my eyebrows expectantly.

"May I spend one last time with you in Cittàcigni?"

It seemed like a harmless request. Maybe he just needed to get this relationship stuff out of his system. I thought it over for a moment then nodded. "Okay, one last time." I cringed inwardly, suddenly thinking that maybe it was a bad idea.

"*Bene*. I have a gig tonight, so let us plan for tomorrow morning. I'll pick you up after eleven."

I forced a smile. "I'll be waiting."

He smiled, got up. "*Arrivederci*, Claudia."

I watched him leave until he was out of sight. *What did I just get myself into?*

CHAPTER 8

STEFANO PICKED ME UP THE NEXT MORNING, dressed casually in a pair of army-green cargo shorts, a T-shirt with a faded, abstract skater logo on the front, and a backward ball cap. He reminded me of the way he looked back in high school. Was that intentional? He certainly didn't look very "duke-ish" to me.

After Stefano joined me in the backseat, Vittorio closed the door and took the wheel. Stefano and I sat some distance away from each other. My body shivered from the cold draft that divided us, and a small part of me wished he would take my hand in his.

No attachments, I reminded myself. I couldn't afford to go backward when I'd gotten so far already and just started to get over him—just a little.

I stared out the window, watching the beautiful landscape, but I glanced out of the corner of my eye at Stefano, to see if he was looking at me. I couldn't tell, but I could see a blur of his face and could only assume that he was looking in my direction. *What's he thinking right now?*

Stop it.

I willed my gaze to focus on the passing countryside. But the silence was killing me, so I finally said without looking at him, "Where are we going?"

"To the *piazza*. How are your feet?"

"They feel fine. They healed pretty quickly. The pain is pretty much gone. I can wear heels again!"

He chuckled. "*Fantastico.* It is such a lovely day outside. How does a walk around the piazza sound?"

Absolutely perfect! "It'll do."

"*Ottimo.*" He paused a beat then looked at me guiltily. "I... would have loved to spend the entire day with you, but unfortunately, I have to attend a meeting with city officials this evening, and then another gig in Alta Rosa."

I shrugged. "Of course." *What was he expecting me to say at this point?*

I turned back to the window, and the silence resumed again. I glimpsed Vittorio in the rearview mirror. He had caught my gaze and quickly looked away. There was a nervous hint in his eyes. *Does he know something I don't?*

We drove into the heart of Cittàcigni and got out at the piazza. Stefano slipped on his sunglasses and looked just like a tourist—or a high school skater boy. Maybe he really *had* done that intentionally in order to remain incognito. *Smart.*

Stefano and Vittorio spoke to each other briefly in Italian, then Vittorio drove off. Stefano turned to me. "He will be back by three o'clock."

I nodded. "That's fine."

He held out his hand to me. I looked at his hand, fighting tooth and nail with myself to not take it. If I did, I would never get over his wonderful touch and lovely warmth. I would never get over him.

So I stared at his hand long and hard, but I didn't take it. He finally lowered his hand and sighed. Hurt and disappointment filled his eyes. He stuffed his hands in his pockets and gestured with a tilt of his head for me to follow.

I walked beside him down the sidewalk, and even that was difficult. I could smell his sandalwood cologne, and I wondered if he was doing that on purpose—little things to make me snap. Well, he was doing a good job of it, but I had to be strong, for my own sake.

The piazza was huge and lined with colorful flowers and neatly trimmed shrubs in the shapes of swans. A giant fountain occupied the center of the piazza, its magnificent spray reaching several feet into the air. There weren't many people out, and most were elderly couples occupying wooden benches that dotted the area. Strips of businesses in rustic-looking buildings surrounded the area, and I suddenly had a feeling of déjà vu. I hoped I didn't run into another one of Stefano's family members who was going to push me into getting another dress.

Then I spotted a vacant building between a quaint sweetshop and a bookstore. There was a sign in the window written in German, French, Italian, and English that said: Rental Space Available. Smiling, I thought about my five-year plan of eventually owning my own gallery where I could showcase and sell my art. This empty space was perfect. I envisioned wood floors, track lighting, brick walls, and all of my art on display. Another section would be designated for teaching private classes. If I could find a place like this back home, I would be all set to live my dream. I took out my phone and snapped a picture of the empty building space.

"What are you doing?" Stefano asked.

I quickly tucked my phone back in my pocket and cleared my throat. "Uh, nothing. Just getting some ideas."

He arched an eyebrow. "Ideas? For what?"

I could tell him, right? I wouldn't be seeing him or this place anymore, so I wouldn't have to worry about him shelling money out to buy that space for me, which, knowing him, he probably would. "I was thinking about building an art studio, and the size of this building's space is perfect."

His eyes lit up. "You want an art studio?"

I smirked. "Before you write that check, the answer is no, I don't want you buying me a studio. I already have everything planned out for what I want to do when I return home. I just needed this picture as reference of what to look for."

His face dulled slightly, and he moistened his lips, probably realizing that I was on to him. "I see."

"It's been my dream to showcase my art, as well as teach it to others. I plan to hold private classes in my studio."

"Oh, Claudia. That is such a wonderful dream. I admire your independence, ambition, and determination. You know your worth, and you know exactly what you want to do with your life. I wish more girls around here were like you." He looked thoughtful for a moment. "I have another favor to ask. Just one more."

I arched my eyebrow at him expectantly.

"Will you… accompany me back to the villa just one last time?"

"What!"

He lowered his head. "I… want my mother to see what a wonderful woman you are. She has been trying to convince me that you are a bad influence, and she thinks you are the cause of my not taking my position seriously. But on the contrary, it is because of you that I feel this need to speak out about change and improving the city to its truest potential."

I fumed. *How dare that woman!* We'd barely met, and she was already judging me. I didn't care if she was the duchess or even the queen. It was time I stood up to "Her Grace," as well. I glared, lifting my head. "I will gladly accompany you and see your mother."

He studied me for a moment then nodded. "*Grazie.*"

Yeah, I'll accompany him, all right. I had a few words to exchange, myself.

We walked around the piazza a bit more then ate a delicious lunch. Five minutes before three o'clock, Vittorio was waiting outside the restaurant, leaning up against the hood of the shiny black sedan while he chatted on his cell. He spotted us as we exited the restaurant, quickly ended his conversation, and opened the back door for us.

During our trip back to Stefano's mansion, I sat on edge, my fingers gripping the seat cushion, as I thought about what I was going to say to Stefano's mother.

"Are you all right, Claudia?" Stefano asked.

I snapped out of my thoughts but didn't acknowledge him. "Yeah, fine."

Stefano pressed a button behind the driver's seat. As the tinted glass window rose between us and the driver's area, Vittorio's eyes turned my way in the rearview mirror then promptly returned to the road.

I was truly alone with Stefano. Chances were, Vittorio wouldn't be able to hear us through the glass partition. I wondered if he could still see us? Or was it one of those one-way windows?

"I still cannot help but make one last conscious effort to try and convince you to stay," Stefano said. "To convince you that I truly love you."

I shook my head slowly. "No, you can't. We're going to talk to your mother, right?"

He nodded. "Sì. After that, I will take you back to the hotel. I still have that meeting with the officials."

"What's the meeting about?"

He shrugged. "Just some issues on improving the city. And improving the local university. There are talks about expanding it."

"That's good. I hope it happens."

The remaining few minutes of our trip were quiet. Before I knew it, we'd pulled up at the mansion's entrance. Vittorio let us out, and Stefano escorted me inside. It was a quarter past three, and a few of the servants were hard at work cleaning and tending to other duties. Stefano asked one of the servants something in Italian, and they pointed him to the main study. There, the duchess sat with two other servants amid a stack of papers. She appeared deep in thought about something as she tapped a ballpoint pen to her lips. It reminded me of the way my dad looked when he was struggling to balance the monthly budget.

The woman before me looked nothing like the supermodel I remembered a few days ago. She wore no makeup, revealing the slight wrinkles around the corners of her eyes and mouth. Her hair was tied in a messy auburn ponytail, and she wore a casual blue-plaid blouse and a pair of black slacks. She actually looked—normal, like a woman in her mid-forties.

One of the servants lifted her head, and I realized she wasn't a servant at all. Hers was the last face I'd expected to see—Mirella. I frowned and looked to Stefano. He looked back at me guiltily. Had he known that she was going to be here? My body went rigid.

Stefano's mother, Mirella, and the servant regarded Stefano and me with a start. Then Mirella and the servant inclined their heads. "*Buon pomeriggio,* Your Grace," they said together.

Stefano inclined his head then waved his hand dismissively at the servant. "Leave us, Enrico."

The servant nodded and quickly left. Stefano turned his attention to Mirella.

Mirella smiled politely to him, then to me. I wanted to convince myself that this wasn't some sort of sick setup by Stefano, but the bad feeling in my gut was getting stronger by the second.

The duchess gave Stefano and me a cool glance, then her face went stony as she stared at her son. She held out a ballpoint pen to him as she spoke in Italian to him.

Scowling, Stefano didn't take the pen. "For the last time, Mother, I do not want to hide our conversation from Claudia."

She rolled her eyes and cursed under her breath. "You are going to be the death of me, Stefano Trevisani!"

Mirella whipped her head back and forth, looking from me and Stefano to the woman, then quietly left the room. "*Scusi,*" she whispered, her head lowered.

I looked at Stefano to see if he was watching Mirella leave, but his eyes were focused on his mother at the moment.

"I need to talk to you about something, Mother."

The woman made a face at me then looked back to her son. "Oh? And what would that be? Has this girl been giving you bad advice again?"

I clenched my fists. *Why, you—*

"Actually," he said, "she has given me wonderful advice. It is about expressing my opinions about the city I love. All these stuffy traditions are ruining

Cittàcigni's economy and tourism, especially when it comes to attracting young people. Do you realize almost all the young people leave Cittàcigni and head to Alta Rosa to go to college and start up new businesses? It is a disgrace, Mother. I do not want to be the duke of a sleepy town."

Her eyes narrowed at me, then she focused her attention back to Stefano. "How dare you? Your father and forefathers worked hard to get Cittàcigni the way it is now. You would throw it all away over this silly girl's notions?"

I opened my mouth to protest, but Stefano placed his hand on my shoulder and shook his head, silently signaling to me that he had things under control. I sure hoped he did because I was so ready to tear this woman a new one. "This was not Claudia's idea. This was my own. I miss Father, and I know you still mourn his loss, but I cannot be him, like you want me to be. I am my own person, Mother. I think he would have preferred it that way. I have the goodness of Cittàcigni in mind when I say that this city needs a change."

She crossed her arms. "And what do you intend to do to 'change' things?"

"For one, I am going to approve the proposals for the expansion and upgrades of the university. I want Cittàcigni to have one of the most elite schools in the country. I want it to be a place that would attract only the brightest and most creative minds not just in Cittàcigni, but around the world. I can make things happen fast, and by the time the new school year starts, it would be put in motion.

"I want to encourage creativity among our citizens, especially the youth. I want more art and music programs to be implemented. Anything and everything that inspires creativity, I want it done. This will be the most innovative city in all of Bellacigna. And it will spark up tourism as well as residency. It is just what Cittàcigni needs to get out of this slumping phase. I plan to present all of this at the meeting today."

She tapped her chin in thought, still frowning. "Your words have merit, Stefano, but you are far too reckless. You run around every night at these clubs, playing that awful music, attracting all those uncouth women. Your… 'hobbies' are a conflict of interest as the future duke of Cittàcigni. What are you willing to sacrifice, Stefano?"

"I will sacrifice neither. Had I not been working in the club, I would have never reunited with Claudia." He smiled at me.

Her mouth dropped open slightly. "Reunited? You mean you have known this girl before?"

"Sì. We went to the same high school in Columbia, South Carolina, during Father's seven-month tenure there. Claudia was the only one who bothered talking to me, and even stood up to some of the students who picked on me. I will never forget all that she has done."

I sighed. It had seemed like such a simple gesture at the time. Who would've thought it meant so much to him after so long?

"You were picked on? Why did you not ever tell us this?"

"Because I did not want you or Father making a scene about my status or… 'privileges.' I just wanted to live a normal life like the other kids and meet a normal girl, like Claudia, on my own. Not someone you or Father handpicked."

As tempted as I was to butt in, I kept quiet.

She shook her head. "Stefano, this discussion is over. You will find yourself a nice Bellacignan girl, and not some foreign commoner who knows nothing of our traditions or language."

His nostrils flared. "Mother, if I cannot be with Claudia, then…" He paused, his face growing darker. "Then I will relinquish my title, my status—*everything*—and leave Bellacigna."

My jaw dropped.

The duchess's eyes widened, and her face paled. "You cannot be serious!"

"I am very serious, Mother." He pulled his phone and wallet from his pocket and set them on the desk. "I will not be needing these anymore. I will leave right now. Donate all my clothes, money, and personal items to charity."

This is unreal. I wanted to tell him that he was insane. The words were on the tip of my tongue, but I held them back.

Her hands clenched and unclenched as she stared at the items on the table. Her lips pursed.

Stefano took one step back, looked at his mother sadly, then at me. "Come, Claudia. I will take you back to your hotel." He spun and headed to the door.

I hesitated in following him. I whipped my head back and forth, trying to decide. At that moment, I noticed something sparkling from the woman's cheek. *A tear?*

She swiped up the wallet and phone and swept across the room, catching up to him as he opened the door. "Stefano…"

He paused.

She heaved a huge sigh. "Do not leave, son. Maybe you are right. The city could do well with some change."

His hand slipped away from the door handle, and he looked over his shoulder at his mother.

Her gaze bounced from him to me, then back to him. "I can see how much Claudia means to you, and it is obvious that you are in love with her, but… does Claudia feel the same way about you?"

Stefano opened his mouth to say something, then he quickly closed it and turned to me. His face was pale.

I like him, but I'm convinced that a relationship will never work. I searched for the right words. "He's a good friend, er… Your Grace. I'm flattered that he loves me so, but unfortunately, this is the last time we will see each other. I'm heading back to America soon." I smiled slightly, trying to make light of this rather morose conversation. "I would still like it if you joined me for the trip back to the hotel, Stefano."

His eyes dulled. His mouth twitched as though he were trying to smile, but he failed miserably. "Sì."

His mother nodded and frowned. "I see. Well, that is very unfortunate." She turned to Stefano. "I think it is time you took your rightful place. You have a strong ambition, like your father had. I will trust you will make Cittàcigni the best it can be." Smiling slightly, she handed him his wallet and phone, which he took and slipped back into his pocket.

I raised my eyebrows. I think it was the first time I'd ever seen her smile. And it was a lovely one.

She acknowledged me. "Forgive me, Signorina Claudia, for my behavior and for misjudging you. I was worried for my only son, since he has such a large responsibility following the unexpected death of his father. Our country has never been the same since. I hope you understand."

I lifted my head slightly. *An apology? From the duchess? Unreal.* "I accept your apology." I looked at Stefano, hoping he would take my hint that I was ready to leave.

"*Grazie* for understanding, Mother." He gestured to me. "Let us go." He turned and headed for the door.

We walked in silence, and the few servants we passed gave us the briefest of glances. I took one last look around each of the halls we passed through, trying to remember this place forever.

Movement in my peripheral vision drew my attention to a nearby room with the door slightly ajar. I could make out two figures beyond. I stopped and looked at one of the figures. *Is that Vittorio?*

"Hey," I said, grabbing Stefano gently by the back of the arm.

Stefano stopped and looked over his shoulder at me. "What is it?"

"Vittorio is driving us back, right?"

Stefano's brow wrinkled slightly, then he tilted his head to the side. "Sì. Why do you ask?"

I pointed to the slightly open door. "I thought I just saw him in there."

One of his eyebrows rose. "The storage area? Why would he be in there?" He approached the door and creaked it open. Light from the room's tiny window fell upon two people in a liplock.

"Mirella? Vittorio?" Stefano asked.

The two jumped and quickly pulled away from their kiss. Mirella's face grew beet red, and Vittorio lowered his head, ashamed.

"Forgive us, Your Grace!" the two said simultaneously.

Stefano's face hardened as he stared at the two of them for several moments. Then his body shook, and he threw his head back and laughed loudly.

I watched Stefano for a moment before turning to the couple.

"Sorry? For what?" Stefano said. "I think it is wonderful that you two have finally decided to stop dancing around each other and make things happen."

Mirella quirked a smile. She and Vittorio were holding hands, and I noticed her hand squeeze his a little tighter.

Something in my chest suddenly felt a little lighter, though I felt two feet tall for ever thinking that Stefano had a thing for Mirella. He was right all along. *He really does love me.* But still, I had made up my mind to not get involved. I slipped away from the three and headed for the front entrance.

I overheard Vittorio stammer something in Italian.

"Sì. But I will drive her back," Stefano answered.

Vittorio replied, a tone of shock in his voice, then he paused. A pair of keys jingled afterward.

I looked behind me just in time to see Stefano swipe the keys from Vittorio.

"Have fun, you two," Stefano said over his shoulder. "I look forward to receiving a wedding invitation very soon."

Mirella looked away and covered her mouth, suppressing a giggle.

Stefano passed me in the hall and started for the front door. "Now, then. Where were we?"

I lifted my eyebrows. "So you're going to drive me?"

"Sì."

"I've never seen you drive before. Do you even know *how?*"

He chuckled. "Of course I can. What? You do not think dukes know how to drive?"

My gaze shifted. "Well I didn't say *that*, but…" Before I could finish my thought, Stefano held the front door open for me.

"If this is going to be the last time I will see you, then I want to make every moment count," he said with a serious edge to his tone.

I headed outside. He saw me to the passenger-side door, and then climbed into the driver's seat.

Yeah, this will be our last day together. And tomorrow, I will awaken from this dream…

The taxi arrived at the airport a few miles from Alta Rosa, and with my ticket and bags in tow, I made my way to the departure gate. The walls throughout the airport displayed framed landscapes of scenic spots around Bellacigna. I tried not to pay attention to them because it made my heart ache. Every time I saw snippets of the beautiful country, I couldn't help but think about Stefano. And that was the last thing I needed. The vacation was officially over, and I needed to return to my simple old life—which didn't involve royalty. I already had everything planned as soon as I got home: say hello to my folks, find an apartment, then start job-hunting. Thankfully, there was no Stefano anywhere in that list.

Sitting in the waiting area, I played a game of solitaire on my phone then indulged in a romance novel. I unblocked Stefano's number, secretly hoping that he would text me, but he didn't. Well, I'd told him not to contact me anymore. At least he remained true to his word.

My flight was soon announced, and I got ready to board. I couldn't help but take one last peek of the landscape outside the giant glass window before handing my ticket to the attendant and stepping onto the Jetway.

Goodbye, Stefano…

CHAPTER 9

As soon as I landed back in Columbia, time seemed to go into overdrive. I spent some time with my family and met up with Trina. By the end of the week, I'd found myself a cheap furnished studio apartment.

It was nine o'clock at night, and as I sipped on a tall glass of sweet tea, I perused the many artist job openings in and around the city. I had so many choices, but occasionally, thoughts of high school drifted to the forefront of my mind.

I recalled seeing Stefano sitting all alone during lunch period, crafting amazing pencil sketches of faraway places... *Stefano's thousands of miles away now, so stop thinking about him!*

Finally, I willed myself to end my job search at a stopping point and closed the laptop. I lost track of how many jobs I'd applied for, but I was confident one of them would respond. Only time would tell. I had six months to find something.

Falling asleep in my brand-new apartment for the first time felt awkward, maybe because the futon was a lot harder than the soft featherbeds at the Bellacignan lodges and hotels. As I closed my eyes, *he* popped up again—that man who'd been haunting me like a bad dream.

But he was anything *but* bad.

The month that had passed was full of rejection after rejection. After receiving so many, I dreaded turning on the computer. My eyes casually glazed over the endless streams of unread e-mails that all started with "Thank you for submitting to..." I'd read enough of them to know what the rest of that sentence said. Sighing, I called Trina. The phone barely rang a second time before she suddenly picked up.

"Did he propose yet?" she asked, foregoing the greetings amid the background sounds of a noisy coffee shop.

I snorted. "What kind of phone greeting is that?"

"An important one when handsome Bellacignan dukes are involved."

I rolled my eyes. "It's been a month, and I'm so over Stefano."

"Mmmhm."

Sensing her sarcasm, I steered the conversation into the direction I'd originally intended. "Look, Trina. My current job situation isn't looking too bright, and I could really use a cappuccino right about now. Think you can hook me up?"

"Yeah, sure. Come on down, and we can talk."

"Thanks." We said our goodbyes and ended the call. I slipped on a pair of shorts and a tank top then walked down to All-Star Java, which was only four blocks away from my apartment.

Entering the small, quaint coffee shop, I was met with the afternoon lunch crowd, and there was no place to sit. I spotted Trina, who was hard at work behind the counter with the other baristas, handling the seemingly endless orders. I hung out and claimed the first table that opened up. Figuring it would be a while before Trina would be free, I made use of my time by sorting through the e-mails on my phone. After peeking at each of them, I sent them in the trash with the other rejections. Dark thoughts invaded my mind. *I wasn't good enough.* Job recruiters criticized my portfolio, many classifying it as being amateur at best, which was the last thing any aspiring artist wanted to hear.

"Hey, you." The closeness of Trina's voice broke me out of my thoughts. I looked up to find her standing at my table. She smiled and handed me a small cup of cappuccino, complete with a heart design made with the milk in the special way only she knew how to do.

Smiling, I took the cup from her. "Hi, and thanks."

She planted herself in the seat across from me. "Things have slowed down for now. I have about five minutes to spare. So what's up?"

I sighed. "I just need some comforting. Maybe a little advice. I got rejected from all the jobs I applied for."

Her eyes grew wide. "What! You can't be serious. Are you sure you applied everywhere around here?"

I nodded, sipping my drink. "As many as I could find. Most said my portfolio wasn't good enough.

Others were looking for five years or more of professional experience and other nonsense."

"They're asking for five years' experience for an *entry-level* job? That's insane!"

"You're preaching to the choir here. Doesn't make any sense at all."

She tapped her chin in thought. "Maybe you should consider places down in Charleston. Are you willing to relocate?"

"Ehh… I'd rather stay in Columbia if I can help it, but I guess if it's my dream job and the price is right…" I took another sip.

"You gotta go where the opportunities are, girl."

"Yeah, I know. But this is home, y'know? I don't want to leave you or the rest of my friends and family."

"Huh. Well, I'm saving up enough money to vacation in Bellacigna and get swept up by a hot duke. Or maybe even a prince. And when I get married, so long, Columbia!"

I raised my eyebrows at her. "Really? You'd leave me?"

"Of course not! Because I know you'll be right back in Bellacigna soon enough, looking for Stefano again." She smirked.

I stared at her with my mouth open. "Now wait a—"

"I gotta head back to work now. Good luck, girl. You know I'll support you in whatever decision you make." Her smirk never leaving her face, she got up from her chair and headed back behind the counter.

I rubbed the edges of my cup as I thought about her words. *Maybe she knows me better than I think I know myself...*

Another month passed with more of the same rejections because of my "amateurish" portfolio and lack of real-world experience. I couldn't afford to relocate to Charleston with my apartment's six-month lease, so I was seriously considering asking Trina to hook me up with a job at the coffee shop. She was a true friend for supporting me during these hard times, though it didn't come without a price of her constantly asking me about Stefano. Despite it all, I stood firm. There was nothing to say about him. Nothing at all.

But that didn't stop me from thinking about him continuously. I hadn't heard from him in over two months. Perhaps he had truly moved on with his life, as I had hoped. I needed to do the same.

At seven at night, I sat on the couch, flipping through TV channels and trying to de-stress after a long day and think of ways to improve my portfolio. I flipped through an endless display of colors, making my eyes grow heavy. Then before I realized it, I'd fallen asleep.

"And in international news, Duke Stefano Trevisani of Cittàcigni has announced a massive breakthrough for the ever-growing Bellacignan city…"

Either I was dreaming, or I really had heard Stefano's name. I forced my eyes open then squinted at the TV's bright glare. There, on the screen, was Stefano in a formal suit, speaking from behind a podium surrounded by a massive crowd. I was fully awake now.

"This is, indeed, a great change for our city, and I am excited to see what wonderful talents our prestigious school acquires," Stefano announced. Below him was the headline: "The Duke of Cittàcigni funds 12.3 million to city's university."

I sat up straighter and listened to the news anchor continue with the story. Cittàcigni's university was completely revamping its art and music programs. There were plans to offer courses in audio mixing, production, and deejaying. And in the art department...

My eyes widened. Stefano had invited artists from all over the world to teach at the university for a hefty salary. Some of the greats included popular interior designer Paul Lessaire from the Home and Garden channel and Rachel Frankson, a famous sculptress from the UK. My jaw dropped at the list of people who were planning to become faculty there. I knew every one of them. They had each been part of my motivation and inspiration to do what I love.

And Stefano had managed to single-handedly gather them all in one place.

I exhaled. *What I wouldn't do to be able to work among the greats.* But they were great for a reason. I could never hold a candle to them and all they'd accomplished. I was a nobody.

Pushing aside my thoughts, I turned off the TV and opened my laptop. *Might as well clean out my inbox of more waiting rejections.* My finger automatically hit Delete on the rejections, but I stopped when I came across an e-mail from a sender under the name of "International Studies and Affairs Liaison." My brow pinched. It looked legit, but I had a strange feeling it was junk mail. But my curiosity got the better of me, and I opened the message and read carefully.

The letter, addressed to me, was actually an invitation to teach art at Cittàcigni University. I gasped. *An art teaching job? Is this for real?* The letter detailed all the amenities, as well as salary information—which was three times more than what the jobs I'd applied for were offering. The university would pay for my relocation expenses. The liaison's signature was followed by her contact information.

An opportunity to teach art among the greats at the university. It was a dream come true, but was I ready to make this big step and move to Bellacigna?

Stefano. I suspected that the love-struck duke had probably done something outrageous. Who was *really* the International Studies and Affairs Liaison?

My cell suddenly buzzed, and I started. Checking the number, I noticed it was Trina. I exhaled in relief. "Hey."

"Hey, girl! I just saw Stefano on TV!"

I cringed. "Yeah, I saw him, too."

"Geez. He looked so hot in that suit."

"He looked all right…"

Trina snorted. "Quit trying to convince yourself out of loving him. You want him so bad, you don't even know what to do with yourself."

"I like him, Trina. But I don't know if I want to spend the rest of my life with him." I paused. "Hey, I got this e-mail…" I filled her in on the details.

"Are you serious? Wow, I had no idea that, uh…"

I arched an eyebrow. "No idea that what?"

"Uh, well, you know… I, um…"

"Say it!"

"All right. Don't get upset. I was just trying to help. After we had that talk last month, I visited the Careers section on Cittàcigni University's website and saw that they were looking for art teachers, so I filled out an application on your behalf."

"You *what!*" The phone nearly slipped from my ear.

"It was a perfect opportunity, Claudia! I couldn't resist. Now it's official—you have a job, *and* the man of your dreams is waiting for you."

I swallowed a bitter taste in my mouth. I should've known she was behind this somehow. "What if I get there and things don't work out with the job? Or with Stefano? I'll be stuck halfway across the world with no way back."

"Stuck with all those hot Bellacignan men? One can only dream. Look, Claudia, it's time to leave your safety bubble of familiarity and move on with your life. You're an amazing artist who's fresh out of college. If no one around here will hire you, then it's about time you took your skills elsewhere."

"And what about you? I'll never see you again…"

She laughed. "Oh, don't worry. I'll be sure to come visit you as often as I can. And there's always video chat."

I thought about the options. She was right—I would probably never get another opportunity like this again. And the chance to see Stefano again seemed to really seal the deal. *Who am I fooling to think that man didn't do all sorts of crazy things to me?*

"Go to him, Claudia," Trina said, interrupting my thoughts. "That's an order!"

I smiled and closed my eyes for a moment. Images of short, curly black hair, olive skin, and green eyes looking at me with such passion and emotion flooded my mind. I couldn't let him slip away. I just hoped it wasn't too late.

CHAPTER 10

I'D NEVER THOUGHT I WOULD BE STEPPING OFF the Jetway of the international airport in Alta Rosa again. Traveling across the ocean to live my new life was something I couldn't have imagined doing, but I was. And it helped that I had friends and family who were supportive of the transition. And of course, Trina made me promise that I would make room in my new apartment for her to crash in whenever she visited. As if I could ever say no to my best friend.

Strangely enough, however, I'd not heard anything from Stefano in six months. He hadn't called or e-mailed me, and I wondered if perhaps he was truly done with me. Did he even know that I was moving to Bellacigna? Trina was right, though. There were plenty of other hot Bellacignan men. I couldn't keep dwelling on something that was never meant to be.

I was making my way through the airport, which was busy with early-morning commuters, following the signs to the baggage claim area, when I noticed a familiar man in a black chauffeur's outfit standing at the exit. He was holding up a sign with my name written on it. I did a double take then smiled.

"Vittorio!" I waved.

The man looked in my direction, then a bright smile lit his face. Approaching me, he folded the sign and tucked it in a pocket of his coat. "Ah! *Buongiorno*, Signorina Gray!"

Something glinted on his left hand, and I realized it was a silver ring—a wedding band. My smile grew. "Oh my gosh! Did you and Mirella finally tie the knot?"

Vittorio beamed. "Sì, not long after you left. It was a fabulous wedding hosted at the royal mansion."

"Congratulations. I can't believe I'm back here again."

"His Grace has also been excited for your arrival."

Another wave of happiness swept through me. "Is Stefano waiting in the car?"

"No, not this time. He had a few engagements at the university to tend to. I am afraid that he will be busy all day." He walked through the exit and gestured for me to follow.

His words brought a slight twinge of disappointment in my gut as I joined him outside. But then the feeling went away when I suddenly realized that we were leaving the airport without my luggage. "Hey, wait. I have a bunch of stuff to get from baggage claim."

Vittorio shook his head. "No need to worry, signorina. All of your items will be waiting for you at your new home."

I blinked. "Home? As in an actual *house?* I thought I was getting an apartment."

"You have been upgraded as per special request by His Grace."

I bit my bottom lip. So it seemed that Stefano still had his best interests in mind for me. *He hasn't changed after all these months.*

Vittorio helped me into the backseat of the sedan, then he slid into the driver's seat.

An hour later, we pulled up along the curb of a narrow road in front of a two-story mid-sized house amid a group of cypress trees. The house's exterior had a rustic feel to it with its ornate red-tiled hipped roof. The second-floor windows had tiny balconies lined with wrought-iron railings, and an intricately carved stone archway surrounded the front door and first-floor windows. A stone railing wrapped around the front of the house, creating a small porch area. Thick vines grew along decorative brackets that supported the overhanging boxed eaves.

Vittorio opened the back passenger door. Stepping out the car, I continued ogling the house, and I inhaled a fragrant, sweet smell of moonflower blossoms that lined the cobblestone walkway.

"This is where I'm staying?" I asked Vittorio.

He nodded. "Sì. Is it to your liking?"

I grinned. "Are you kidding? I *love* it! Does this mean I'm going to be neighbors with Paul Lessaire?" I looked down the street at the other houses.

Vittorio tilted his head. "Ah… perhaps. I believe Signor Lessaire stays about ten *minuti* from here."

"Oh." I deflated a little. Still, Mr. Lessaire would be my colleague, and I was sure to see him often at the university. "So… I take it this house is all Stefano's doing?"

"Ah… sì…" Vittorio paused and looked at the ground as if he were fishing for the right words.

Finally, he looked up. "Signorina Gray, Stefano has been... quite sad since you left months ago. But he's been more determined than ever to work harder and achieve his dreams, like the university. However, each time I see him, I can still sense the emptiness in him. He misses you. He *loves* you."

I took a deep breath. "Y-Yeah..." I bit my bottom lip. "But our worlds are vastly different. I'm sure Stefano is always busy, being the duke and all. He probably never has time for relationships."

Vittorio smiled. "On the contrary, Stefano prefers living a simple life. We have talked many times. He has been very responsible with his duties ever since his position as duke was made official, and he feels confident that he would be able to balance his life and still give the woman he loves the love and attention she deserves. I trust his judgment. And I hope that you can trust Stefano that he will always keep you happy."

I thought about all the wonderful gestures and things Stefano had said and done for me. His words seemed to come from his heart, and I really couldn't find a reason to doubt him.

Vittorio showed me to the front door. He opened it with an ornate silver key and held the door open for me to pass. The smell of new wood and furniture drew me in. The place was just as beautiful on the inside as it was on the outside. Though it looked deceivingly bigger on the outside, the interior was just the right size for me.

My luggage and moving boxes were gathered in the living area, ready to be unpacked. Vittorio walked me through the house, giving me a quick tour. We ended in the kitchen. On the dinette table was a brown-paper-wrapped box with a handwritten note attached. I picked up the note, which I could tell was Stefano's handwriting.

Dear Claudia, Please do not open this until we meet again. -Stefano

I took another look at the box. It wasn't small, so jewelry—such as a ring—was out of the question, thank goodness. *Stop kidding yourself.* Part of me had been secretly hoping that he would pop the question, but I wasn't holding my breath. He might love me, but he was still a busy man, and marriage was probably the last thing he wanted to add to his plate right at that moment.

I looked up at Vittorio, who looked back at me, amused with his hands behind his back.

I furrowed my brow. "You know what's in this box, don't you?"

He grinned. "I am not authorized to say."

I rolled my eyes. "Of course you're not."

"Would you like me to inform His Grace that you are here?"

"Yeah, that'll be fine."

"All right." He took out his phone and dialed a number. After a few minutes of speaking in Italian, Vittorio ended the call and nodded to me. "He will be by in a few hours. Do you need anything before I leave, signorina?"

"No, I think that's all." I raised my eyebrows. "So did Stefano buy you and Mirella a house, too?"

"Oh, no. We afforded our own. But I find myself frequenting the duchess's villa. She still requires my services from time to time."

We said our farewells, and Vittorio saw himself out.

Around seven o'clock, there was a knock at the front door. I stopped unpacking, dabbed sweat from my brow, and answered it. A shiver ran through me at the sight of Stefano standing there, all decked out in a sports hoodie, a beanie cap, and faded jeans, like a hot urban music star.

He smiled that charming smile that I'd missed so much.

I swallowed once and said in a choked-up voice, "Hi, Stefano."

Stefano said nothing and stepped inside. I couldn't help but take a step back. Slowly, he wrapped his arms around me and pulled me to him. He kissed my forehead, and I closed my eyes.

"Claudia…" he whispered.

I smiled at the sound of my name uttered from his lips.

He tilted my chin up, forcing me to look into his eyes. The pads of his fingers electrified my skin. Slowly, our faces came closer until our lips touched. I melted from his sweet kiss.

Please don't let this moment end.

He held me tighter as he deepened the kiss. I followed his lead, a small moan escaping my lips. Then I had to pull back. It was getting too hot too fast.

He looked at me with kiss-swollen lips and hooded eyes. He caressed the side of my face with his hand. "I have missed you so much, *bella*," he whispered.

I sighed. "I've missed you, too. I'm sorry that I've been a bit flaky about things. I'm just... afraid of what will happen to us."

He inched his face close. "I am afraid, too. But is not true love about taking chances?"

"Yeah." I smiled. "You know, I'm glad I came back. I... I want to stay here with you." I choked out those words.

His face brightened. "That is wonderful news, Claudia. I am so glad." He kissed my lips again. "I love you, Claudia. It broke my heart to see you leave, but I understood and hoped that one day you would return. And that perhaps…" He looked away a moment. "Did you see my note?"

I raised my eyebrows. "The one that said for me not to open until we meet again?"

"Sì."

"Yes, and it's still there where you left it." I led him to the kitchen and showed him the note and package.

He picked up the note, crumpled it, and handed me the box. "Okay. Well, you can open it now."

I looked at the box in my hands. My heart was pounding, and I didn't know why. I gave it a little shake, but I couldn't hear anything inside. I looked at him again, and he looked back at me, eager and patient.

I undid the bow on the box and peeked inside.

"A box inside of a box?" I lifted an eyebrow.

He smirked. "Open it."

And so I did. Inside that was an even smaller box. I had to laugh this time. "You're leaving me in suspense, Stefano."

He laughed, too. "Keep opening them."

After about five more boxes, I reached a really small box made of dark-blue velvet. "I hope this is the last one."

He said nothing and continued smiling.

It didn't seem to have another box inside, so I held my breath and popped open the top. My heart stopped. A shiny diamond ring glinted back at me. I blinked several times, wondering if what I was seeing was real. My hand began to shake, and the glittering of the diamond increased. I suddenly lost feeling in my hand. *No, this can't be.*

Then I felt the warmth of Stefano's hand touch mine. He took the ring out of the box and slipped it on my left ring finger. Still holding my hand in his, he got down on one knee and kissed the back of my hand. His lips hovered there afterward, so close to my skin. His warm breath brushed over my skin as he spoke, sending small shivers up and down my spine.

"Claudia," he whispered. "I love you. I want to spend my life with you. Since the day we first met in high school, I dreamed that I would one day meet you again. I would love it if you accepted my hand in marriage so that we can live happy together, teaching the arts, music, and doing what we love to do. So, what do you say, *bella?* Will you marry me?"

My cheeks hurt from smiling so hard. I couldn't believe what was happening. But the first thing that came out of my mouth was "Yes!"

Stefano beamed. He kissed the ring on my finger and stood back up. "This is the happiest day of my life, and I hope it is for you, too."

I nodded. *More than you know.*

Trina Mauer wins a vacation of a lifetime to the beautiful and luxurious country of Bellacigna. But luck is not the only thing that finds her—so does her love of music and the interest of a cute drummer, Samuele Trevisani. When their worlds collide, and a high-profile music agent comes to town, Trina will have to decide of she's ready to live the band life again, or move on from her past.

Please see the next page for a preview of

Royal Secret

I'M HERE. I CAN'T BELIEVE IT.

I was just a small-town South Carolina girl who always had big dreams. But who knew dreams could ever become real? Mine had come to life in the form of an online ten-day vacation giveaway and a handsome six-foot-four hunk named Erudito, who wore a classy chauffeur's outfit. *"Trina Mauer Vacations in Style"—sounds like the next big-hit television series.* I grinned at the thought.

From under the brim of his black chauffeur's hat, Erudito stared at me in the rearview mirror with enticing brown eyes. As soon as our eyes met, his gaze returned to the road.

I inhaled the rich scent of leather as I ran my hand across the soft upholstery of the limousine's backseat. Last year, I'd told my best friend, Claudia Gray, that we would see each other again soon. *Who knew it'd be* this *soon?* Needless to say, Claudia was just as ecstatic as I was when I told her that I'd won the two-week getaway to Bellacigna sponsored by my favorite romance author, international bestseller M.E. Stacson.

The ride from the airport offered a magnificent view of Bellacigna's picturesque countryside. Claudia had described it as something straight out of a storybook. She wasn't kidding. The trees, full and vibrantly green, stood among endless fields of colorful wildflowers, small farms, and rustic, Italian-style vineyards. My hotel was located in Fiore Luna, a city located thirty miles from the airport and about fifteen minutes from the city of Cittàcigni, where Claudia and her husband, Stefano, lived. Luck would have it that she'd gotten hitched to a handsome Bellacignan like Stefano Trevisani—who also happened to be a *royal duke* in disguise. I wished my life was half as exciting as hers. But not much excitement happened to a barista at a small-town mom-and-pop coffee shop from eight to five.

As we rode into Fiore Luna's outskirts, the top of a giant skyscraper came into view, stretching high above all the others, making it one of the tallest points in the city. The building's windows glittered, reflecting the sun like hundreds of little stars on a pillar. I would've never pegged it for a hotel if I hadn't noticed the impressive gold-plated sign out front that read Verde Suites.

"Whoa! *This* is where I'm staying?" My voice squeaked.

Erudito's eyes met mine again in the rearview mirror. "*Sì, signorina.* Verde Suites is Fiore Luna's premier five-star hotel."

I blinked several times. *I must be dreaming.* I pinched myself just to make sure... nope. The situation was definitely as real as things got. I took a deep breath to calm my nerves. "So what do you recommend I see or do while I'm here, Erudito?"

His brown eyes flicked to mine, the corners wrinkling slightly as he smiled. "*Gelaterie* are a popular thing in this country. Fiore Luna has a really good one about five blocks from your hotel. You should really try the *Di Martina Migliori.* It is a rich chocolate flavor. Very popular."

I raised an eyebrow. "Really? A chocolate gelato is all the rage around here? I won't believe it till I see it—er, taste it."

"Would you like me to drive you there now, signorina?"

While chocolate gelato sounded tempting, it was best that I checked in at the hotel and got settled first. Perhaps I would try to make it to a *gelaterie* sometime the next day, during one of the few breaks in my almost-full schedule. I'd blocked out a lot of time in my planner for sightseeing and activities. Two weeks definitely wasn't long enough to see and do everything. "No, I really should check in to the hotel instead."

"Of course."

I glanced out the window at the strip of quaint shops and cafés that we passed. "How's the nightlife here?"

"Quite lively, signorina. The most popular hotspots are the local jazz lounges."

That certainly piqued my interest. "Really? I love jazz. Any places close by?"

"Sì. There is one just a block from the hotel called Heaven and Blues. Feel free to call me if you would like me to drive you there."

I fingered the business card in my purse, the one Erudito had given me when he'd picked me up at the airport. I would feel awkward calling a chauffeur to drive me one block. Though I had no intentions of bothering him like that, I kept the thought in mind that he would be at my beck and call for the duration of my stay.

Erudito pulled up to the hotel entrance, and two attendants rushed to the car. One carried a sign with the letter *T* written in fancy calligraphy and set it in front of the car. Erudito jumped out and hustled around to open the door for me. I took his offered hand and got out of the car with exaggerated grace, like the red carpet celebrities do—because I had *always* wanted to do that. The attendants loaded my two large suitcases and garment bag onto a fancy gold luggage cart and quickly wheeled it inside the hotel.

"Signorina." Erudito's voice was so close to my ear that I started. He gestured toward the main entrance, and after one glance back at the parked limo, I headed for the doors.

"Why did the hotel staff put a sign in front of the car like that?" I asked, feeling totally clueless.

He walked just a few steps behind me. "It is used by the Trevisani family to denote that the space is reserved."

I halted before the entrance. *Trevisani*. "Did you say Trevisani? As in the Trevisani Royals of Bellacigna?"

"Sì. Though you are not of the royal family, I was instructed to ensure that the sign was placed out."

More questions swarmed through my head, but before I could ask anything else, Erudito gestured for me to continue inside. I was only a few steps away from the revolving glass door when my foot caught on the doorstep. My body pitched forward toward the door, and my heart dropped in my gut as I struggled to keep my balance. I yelped, but the anticipated painful impact never came. Instead, a strong arm grabbed me and pulled me away from the revolving door just as one of them whooshed inches past my face. The smell of leather with undertones of cedarwood touched my senses. I felt Erudito's warmth and rigid body as he steadied me. I put my hand over his for support and stared down at the beautiful contrast of my sandy-brown skin complementing his olive complexion. My cheeks burned. *Great. Erudito must think I'm the biggest klutz now.*

"Are you okay?" he asked in a soft, concerned voice.

I swallowed and nodded, unable to speak.

"Do be careful, signorina," he said, gently steadying me on my feet.

"Thank you," I managed to whisper.

He released me. "I will inform the management of that hazardous step." He led the way inside this time, scanning the area for any more hazards, and I followed.

Stepping through the revolving doors was like stepping through a portal to a magical castle. Glittering chandeliers sent tiny dots of rainbow-colored light dancing about the floor and cream-colored walls of the massive lobby. The blue-marble floors shone like glass despite the constant traffic of hotel guests and workers.

The lobby opened up into a massive atrium that extended above and beyond what my eyes could see. Glass elevators on both ends of the atrium provided access to the many floors above. My mouth hung open as I ogled. If I wasn't careful, I would drool on this expensive-looking floor.

After I checked in, a well-dressed bellhop approached me. He was young, charming, and smiling as though he really loved his job. "*Buonasera*, Signorina Mauer. I will show you to your room." He gestured to the elevators with his white-gloved hand. "*Da questa parte, per favore.*"

I started to follow then stopped and looked over my shoulder at Erudito, who'd stayed behind. He looked up from his conversation with one of the hotel staff and met my gaze. After a final word to the attendant, he joined me. "Is everything all right, signorina?" He glanced at the bellhop, who stood patiently by the elevators, then back at me.

I smiled. The man was nothing short of professional, so professional I had to wonder what he ever did for fun. "Yes, everything's fine." I paused and suddenly realized— "Oh! I should give you a tip. I'm so sorry." I rummaged in my purse for my money envelope. *Geez, how much am I supposed to tip this guy? Twenty euros? Fifty?*

Shaking his head, he waved his hand. "No, signorina. Do not feel obliged to tip. It is my pleasure and duty to assist you." He bowed his head as he tipped his hat. "Please do not hesitate to contact me if you need anything at all. *Arrivederci*. Enjoy your time here in Fiore Luna."

He left, and I stared long and hard at him until he exited the building. *No tip? Is he for real?* The man was too generous for words—and he was just the chauffeur!

I joined the bellhop at the elevators and gave him an apologetic smile. He called an elevator with a push of a button. We rode up to the forty-third floor, and my ears popped because we were so high. The doors swished open, and the plush red-carpeted hallway we stepped out onto stretched toward giant windows at each end. Soft light glowing from silver wall sconces created a cozy, serene atmosphere. The bellhop escorted me to room 4302 and opened the door.

My heart stopped. The room wasn't a suite; it was a *house*—no, a *mansion!* From the stately, elegant mahogany furniture in the living room to the giant island kitchen that looked like something straight out of one of those home-improvement shows on television, everything was sleek and classy, and it made me want to never leave. *This contest had to cost Ms. Stacson a fortune.* But then I remembered she was probably pretty well off from all of her bestselling books. The suite was probably mere pennies for her.

The bellhop gave me a short tour of the place, showing me where everything was and how things worked. We entered the master bedroom, and my jaw dropped. I couldn't get over its sheer size, which was ten times the size of my own bedroom. The giant bed looked like two king-size beds put together. The bathroom was crafted in beautiful, gleaming white marble. A basket full of bath supplies tied with a pink bow sat next to a Jacuzzi that looked big enough to fit five people. My luggage was neatly stowed on a gold shelf in the master bedroom's giant walk-in closet, and my garment bag hung from a matching gold clothes rack.

We ended the tour back at the foyer. "Signorina Mauer, is there anything else you need before I go?" the bellhop asked with a small twinkle in his eye.

I smiled, pegging the question as him wanting a tip. "No, that's all. Thank you very much." I placed a ten-euro note in his hand.

His face brightened, and he quietly slipped it into his pocket. "*Grazie.* Enjoy your stay at the Verde Suites." He tapped the brim of his hat then left.

Alone, I exhaled a huge sigh. My nerves still buzzing, I returned to the bathroom and investigated the Jacuzzi and the basket of items. I was going to make good use of those items in preparation for my night out on the town.

That evening, after a relaxing Jacuzzi bath to calm my nerves, I plopped down on the oversized bed in my nightshirt. I called Claudia from my travel cell, which I'd bought at the airport upon arriving in Bellacigna, to fill her in on my first-day adventures.

"I can't believe you're already having this much fun," Claudia said once I'd finished.

I snorted. "This is nothing compared to your meeting the *Duke* of Cittàcigni." I wondered if Erudito could introduce me to a charming duke. Or maybe even a prince?

"That was just a fluke." Claudia chuckled. "But I believe everything happens for a reason. Who knows? There may be hope for you yet to get hooked up."

"Girl, I wish. But I'm just going to enjoy every ounce of this vacation as much as I can—with or without a royal hunk."

"That's the spirit."

I'd already planned to spend some time hanging out with Claudia during my vacation. We decided on a day and time to meet up for gelato then ended the call. It was eight o'clock—we'd chatted for over an hour. I sprang out of bed, slipped on a strappy little black dress with matching open-toe heels, fixed my hair, then headed out the door.

By nine o'clock, I was standing outside a quaint hole-in-the-wall with the neon Heaven & Blues sign glowing steadily above the entrance. A brawny man in a black suit and tie stood outside the doors with his hands crossed at his waist. He looked my way, inclined his head slightly with a smile, then turned his attention to a group of girls dressed in glitzy outfits and cocktail dresses as he opened the doors for them.

"*Buonasera, signorine,*" he greeted them.

One of the girls responded in honey-toned Italian, and he let out a soft chuckle. The other girls cast flirtatious glances at him as they made their way inside. I followed the group, brushing past the doorman. I couldn't help but take a sidelong look as I passed. His enticing dark-brown eyes were practically boring holes in me. I grinned shyly at him, my cheeks getting hotter as I entered the dimly lit lounge.

The upscale, plush interior swept me away. Red-velvet sofas and chairs provided ample seating everywhere. The wait staff, dressed sharp in black suit jackets and matching bowties, glided silently between tables, carrying trays of drinks.

I claimed a small table to the left of the main stage, where a woman dressed in a long blue cocktail dress sang, accompanied by a pianist and drummer. The table's centerpiece was a red decorative glass jar, which housed a flickering tea candle that created tiny abstract designs on the white tablecloth.

Crossing my legs, I leaned an elbow on the table, my cheek cradled in my hand, and listened to the slow, mellow music. Though I couldn't understand the Italian lyrics, I still vibed out to the classic blues sound.

"*Mi scusi, signorina, vorreste da bere?*"

I blinked out of my trance and looked for the source of the solicitous male voice—an older, thin waiter with cropped salt-and-pepper hair and a matching trimmed beard. He watched me with curious eyes and an amused but charming smile. Unsure of what he was asking, I looked at him with bemusement. "Uh…"

Faint wrinkles creased his face as his smile grew. "Would you like a drink, signorina?"

A drink. I think I'm gonna need several drinks. "Oh, yes, please." My voice cracked.

The waiter looked at me expectantly.

"Ah! Um, I'll have a Pinot Grigio."

"*Ah, ottima scelta.*" He nodded, spun on his heel and headed for the bar.

Applause suddenly came from the crowd. I looked back to the stage in time to see the woman and her band take a bow. A dark curtain closed, and the lights slowly brightened. Much of the audience scattered. Some headed to the restrooms or the bar, while others made their way to the exit. But as quickly as people departed, new faces entered and took over the vacant seats.

The waiter returned with my drink, and I took a sip as the lights dimmed again, cuing the next act. The stage lights transitioned to a cool bluish color, and the curtain opened, revealing a tenor saxophone player, keyboardist, bassist, and drummer. The four men began playing a catchy jazz tune, and the low murmurs among the audience dissipated. When the band had everyone's attention, the sax player—a middle-aged man—stopped playing, and a small spotlight focused on him. While the rest of the band played at a lower volume, he spoke his introduction in Italian. I only understood his name—Vincenzo. He performed a short solo, and the rest of his band accompanied. He gave introductions to the keyboardist and bassist, Castello and Marco, and the spotlight moved to each one in turn as they gave their own solos. The drummer, Samuele, was last, and his introduction was much longer. The spotlight fixed on the man, who looked about my age, sitting behind the drum set. His short black hair was disheveled in just the right way to make my heart leap into my throat as I watched him bust out with his solo, his hands moving across the drums and cymbals with amazing dexterity and timing. Light reflected off the lenses of his black horn-rimmed glasses as he bobbed his head in time to the beat. When he finished, he looked up at the audience, a few stray locks of his hair casually falling across one side of his forehead. A shadow of beard emphasized his square jaw when he smiled. He raised his drumsticks in the air, revealing toned arms beneath the rolled-up sleeves of his plaid button-down shirt. The audience clapped, cheered, and whistled.

Well, I guess when you're that *attractive, you* deserve *massive applause.*

The band continued their set, and all I could do was stare helplessly at that drummer, barely even touching my drink. It wasn't the first time I'd fallen for a guy in a band. I'd made the terrible mistake of getting involved with the guitarist in our little blues band back in college. It hadn't ended well, and I hadn't seen him since.

Listening to the quartet playing classic jazz allowed me to momentarily forget about the bad things in the past. I bobbed my head to the rhythm of the slapping beat of the upright bass and the smooth, rolling tunes of the sax and keyboard. It took me back to my freshman year in college, when my friends and I formed a jazz-and-blues band and did little gigs around town. Claudia had even designed a cute sign for us. We spent the small tips we'd earned on ice cream to celebrate. By my late sophomore year, however, our band had broken up. Sadly, I'd lost touch with them. But that hadn't stopped me from continuing to play my electric bass. At the moment, I regretted not bringing it along.

I'd always hoped to be able to quit my barista job one day and become a full-time professional musician, traveling the world and playing to my heart's content. But I'd convinced myself that it was just a crazy fantasy.

I returned my gaze to the cute drummer, who appeared completely lost in the music. Samuele's eyes were closed, and his head moved while his hands blurred across the drums. It was almost midnight when the band ended their last set. Cheers and applause erupted from the audience, who rose to their feet. The band took a bow, and the curtain closed. The main lights came on again, signaling another intermission in preparation for the next band. Satisfied with an entertaining night, I decided to leave.

Outside, I started for the hotel, feeling physically whipped after such a long day. The jet lag didn't help, either. All I wanted was to enjoy that amazing monster-sized bed waiting for me in my suite. I stared at the line of expensive-looking cars parked along the curb near the building. There were a few more across the street. *This place must really be a hotspot for the rich and famous.*

Approaching a small alley between the lounge and another building, I heard the echo of four male voices. One of them sounded like Vincenzo. I looked toward the voices and spotted three figures illuminated in a bronze wash cast by a lone floodlight attached to a corner of one of the buildings. The men, whom I recognized as the jazz quartet from earlier, gathered near the open trunk of a dark sedan, chatting and laughing. One of the men placed a long instrument case in the trunk then slammed it shut. Samuele stood among them, with a small duffel bag slung over his shoulder.

My heart fluttered at the sight of him, even at a distance. I kept telling myself that I shouldn't be so smitten by a guy I didn't even know, and I willed my feet to continue toward the hotel. The men's voices suddenly stopped, and I glanced over my shoulder. The four of them, including Samuele, were looking in my direction.

My breath caught. *Oh, geez, now they're staring at me!* I whipped around the corner, out of their line of sight, and hugged my back to the wall of the next building. I took several deep breaths in succession, but my nerves were still rattled. Why did the mere sight of him make me act like such a high schooler? They must've all thought I was a weird groupie or something. Embarrassed, I peeled myself off the wall and walked away as quickly as my three-inch heels could take me.

Headlights shone from behind me. I didn't think much of it because of the light traffic, so I continued walking. One of the shiny, expensive cars I'd seen earlier—a white, gleaming sports car—pulled up beside me, matching my pace. I halted, and so did the car. I looked warily toward the dark-tinted window of the driver's side, but I couldn't discern anything beyond. The window slid down, and I got a good look at the driver. Time suddenly stopped.

"*Mi scusi, signorina. Si è persa?*" Samuele asked, his face filled with concern.

I simply stared at him, dumbfounded. He was apparently alone.

"Are you lost? Do you require help?" he asked again.

I blinked when he spoke in accented English. He sounded sincere enough, but my nerves were still on edge. "Oh, n-no, I'm fine. Thanks."

His head tilted slightly, and his brow furrowed. "You were at Heaven and Blues tonight, were you not?"

"Yeah, I was there. I really enjoyed your show. You're an amazing drummer."

He beamed. "*Grazie.* I am glad you enjoyed the show." He paused a beat then said, "My name is Samuele. It is a pleasure to meet you."

Hearing him utter his own name etched it into my mind. "Hi, Samuele. I'm Trina. Nice to meet you, too." I fidgeted with the strap of my purse, feeling torn because part of me said I should leave, but another part of me told me to stay and prolong the meeting just a little while longer. My rational side lost the battle when an idea suddenly came to mind. "Um, I know this is going to sound weird but..." I pulled my planner and a pen from my purse. "Can you autograph my planner?"

He gave me a funny look, probably thinking I was a serious nutcase. Maybe I was, being all starstruck like some rabid groupie. But stuff like that must happen to him all the time. I could only imagine how many women he had clamoring for his attention. Obviously, I was no better.

He adjusted his glasses, and his brow pinched. "Your... planner?"

I nodded and forced a smile, even though I was mentally kicking myself for digging my hole of shame even deeper. But I couldn't help myself. I could stare at this gorgeous Adonis forever.

I'd expected him to make a typical polite excuse that celebrities made whenever they wanted to get away from pests like me. But instead, Samuele parallel parked along the curb and got out. My legs turned to jelly, and my heart beat faster. He had a tall, lean physique and still showed off those beautifully defined forearms beneath his rolled-up shirtsleeves. When he got close, I could see the bright-emerald green of his eyes. I bit my bottom lip and showed him my Erica Collinger–brand planner that I took everywhere. I cherished the little book, with my daily life's precious schedule inscribed on its colorful sticker-and-washi-taped pages.

He looked at it for a moment then laughed. "Oh! I have a sister who is into that sort of thing. I do not understand its appeal." He took the planner and pen then signed the inside cover.

I chuckled. "Just a secret passion of mine." As he handed the planner back, I noticed on his right middle finger was a silver ring with a small crest in the inset. "Thanks for autographing it," I continued, then flipped open the cover to see what he'd written.

"Vivere per la musica. Samuele." I looked back at him. "What does this mean?"

His face softened. "It means 'live for the music,' *bella.*"

A man after my own heart. "I live it all the time. Especially jazz and blues. I played with a group back in college."

"Oh? What did you play?"

"Electric bass. Fun times."

His eyebrows rose. "*Stupefacente!* I have never met a girl who plays the bass."

I blushed. "Really? Well, I guess now you can say you have."

"Do you still play?"

"Yeah, but more for myself, now. Sometimes, I miss playing with the group."

He checked his watch. "Forgive me, *bella.* I must be going now. I hope I will see you again soon."

I sighed. *Of course he has to go. Other obligations, like perhaps a significant other.* "Yeah... I guess I shouldn't hold you up any more. I'd love to check out more of your upcoming gigs, though."

He flashed a warm and bright smile that could melt ice cream. "That would be great. I will be at *Due Passi Salotto* in Cittàcigni this Friday, at eight o'clock."

A quick check of my planner showed that time slot was empty—thank goodness. Most of my sightseeing was planned during the day. He gave me the details, and I quickly jotted down the information. "Thanks. I'll be there."

Samuele's concern returned to his face. "Do you need a lift?"

I sank my teeth into my bottom lip, tempted to say yes, but my rational, cautious side won the battle this time. With a small, disappointed sigh, I shook my head. "Thank you, but there's no need. I'm staying at Verde Suites just down the street." I pointed.

"Okay. Be safe, then, *bella*. I will look for you on Friday night. *Ciao*." He returned to his car.

I waited for him to leave first, but when he didn't, I started toward the hotel. He turned his headlights on, creating an illuminated path all the way down the street. I occasionally looked over my shoulder and noticed he still hadn't budged from his parking spot.

I was only a few yards away from the hotel's entrance when the light faded. I turned again, to wave at him and let him know I was okay, but he was already gone.

ABOUT THE AUTHOR

MARIE LONG is a novelist who enjoys the snowy weather, the mountains, and a cup of hot white chocolate. She's an avid supporter of literacy movements like We Need Diverse Books (WNDB) and National Novel Writing Month (NaNoWriMo). To learn more about her, visit her website: www.marielongauthor.com.

* 9 7 8 0 9 8 6 3 0 1 9 9 5 *